FIERY RED HAIR,
EMERALD GREEN EYES,
AND A VICIOUS IRISH TEMPER

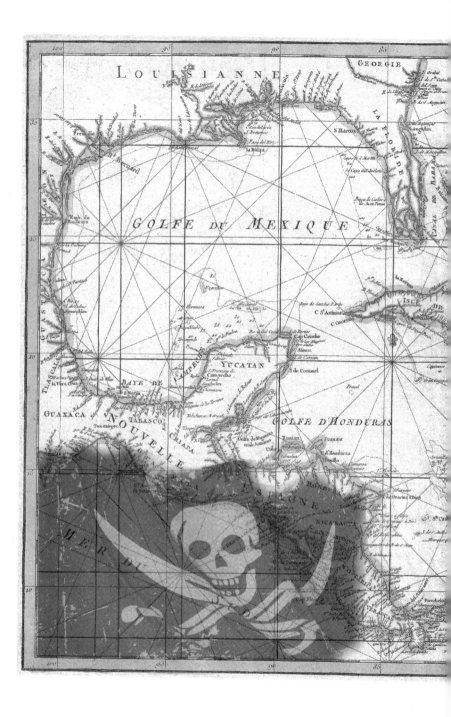

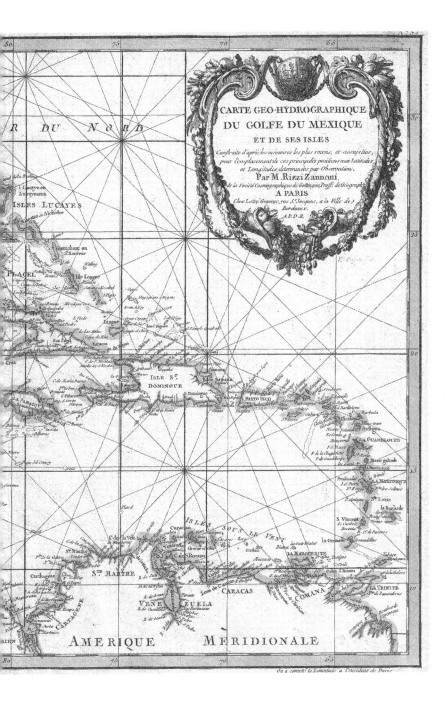

CARTE GEO-HYDROGRAPHIQUE
DU GOLFE DU MEXIQUE
ET DE SES ISLES
Construite d'après les mémoires les plus recens, et assujelies,
pour l'emplacement de ces principales positions aux Latitudes
et Longitudes, determinées par Observation.
Par M. Rizzi Zannoni,
de la Société Cosmographique de Gottingue, Proff. de Géographie.
A PARIS
Chez Lattré Graveur, rue St. Jacques, à la Ville de
Bordeaux.
A.P.D.R.

MR DU NORD

ISLES LUCAYES

PLACEL

ISLE ST.
DOMINGUE

LA JAMAIQUE

PORTO RICO

LA GUADELOUPE

Marie galande
la Dominique
LA MARTINIQUE
Ste. Lucie
la Barbade
S. Vincent
la Grenade
LA MARGUERITE
LA TRINITE

ISLES SOUS LE VENT

Ste. MARTHE

CARTHAGENE

Maracaybo

CARACAS

COMANA

VENEZUELA

AMERIQUE   MÉRIDIONALE

On a compté les Longitudes à l'Occident de Paris.

Fiery Red Hair, Emerald Green Eyes, and a Vicious Irish Temper

The Absolutely True Story of the World's First Female Pirate

RALPH E. JARRELLS

WordCrafts

Fiery Red Hair, Emerald Green Eyes, and a Vicious Irish Temper, although a work of fiction, is based on actual persons and events. The author has endeavored to be respectful to all persons, places, and events presented in this novel, and attempted to be as accurate as possible. Still, this is a novel, and all references to persons, places, and events are fictitious or used fictitiously.

Fiery Red Hair, Emerald Green Eyes, and a Vicious Irish Temper
Copyright © 2019
Ralph E. Jarrells

ISBN: 978-1-948679-64-0
Library of Congress Control Number:2019947986

Cover concept and design by David Warren.

Published by WordCrafts Press
Cody, Wyoming 82414
www.wordcrafts.net

Dedication

First, with my eternal thanks to Pat Hubbard Mullis and Harriette Edmonds, editors—two women that made me look smart and made Mike Parker's job easier.

Second, Mike Parker, publisher extraordinaire. He took a chance on an unknown writer and turned him into an unknown author.

Anne Bonny was a strong woman in history.

This book is dedicated to the strong women in my life. There were many starting with Sybil E. Jarrells.

Any list would be incomplete, so, (with apologies to Willie Nelson:

Here's to you strong, all the strong women I have known before

Foreword

This story was told to me as absolute truth by an elderly English lady following an excellent meal and over a pleasantly hot Irish coffee sitting in front of a crackling, early winter fire. She had spent many years living in Charleston, South Carolina, but had lost none of the etiquette expected from a proper English lady. She was very specific in her descriptions. Since she and her sources are long dead, the reader must be willing to allow the storyteller the benefit of the doubt.

I knew her to be a woman of absolute veracity.

It took over 30 years for my curiosity to grow to the point that I was enticed to delve into the historical events that surround her incredible story. You are welcomed to search, as I did, for verification of the facts contained herein. You may perhaps find more information than I did. You may, perhaps, find different facts. It matters not to me. I now accept the story, as you read it here, as the absolute truth.

I may or may not have changed some of the names in this story. My Southern upbringing taught me it is neither nice nor genteel to divulge family secrets. My grandmother called that "airing the dirty laundry." Another indulgence from my past is the ability to embellish on occasion.

So, here it is; the real story of Anne Bonny—the girl with fiery red hair, emerald green eyes, and a vicious Irish temper—the absolutely true story of the first female pirate, in her own words.

Introduction

I t was 1755.

To say it was unusual for a woman—especially a 56-year-old woman—to own, much less manage a large plantation, would be a gross understatement. Oh, women had their *place*, to be sure. And that *place*, even for the wife of a plantation owner, was only a slight step above the servants and slaves.

Women were created to give birth to children. They were there to oversee the details of running the house. They were there, in some cases, to add wealth to their husbands as a part of their dowry. But they were not to be taken seriously. Not in the eyes of men.

Anne Cormac was the exception. But then, she was the exception to most rules for women in the 1700s.

The silver-haired woman owned and operated Goose Creek Plantation. She owned the plantation in the same way she owned the space she occupied. And that was never in doubt. Goose Creek Plantation was 400 acres of prime high land located on the river for which it was named. It produced fine, long-strand cotton, a substantial indigo crop, and enough animals and vegetables to feed her household and all of the slaves who worked the land.

The high land was separated from the river by almost a hundred acres of impounded marshland that provided the plantation's primary, *legitimate* means for income—rice fields. The rice, indigo, and cotton alone would have made

Goose Creek Plantation's owner among the richest in the low country of South Carolina. However, it was Anne Cormac's *sideline* that made the successful operation of the plantation, her generous philanthropy, and any number of other business endeavors possible. Anne Cormac was an occasional buccaneer, and buccaneering generated substantial capital for her, her businesses, her notable charity, and her community enrichment projects.

Miss Anne, as she was known, was a fixture in the society of Charles Town. She was rumored to be the money behind more than one of the local banks, a substantial number of the factors who managed much of the trade through the Charles Town port, and the driving influence in the development of Charles Town's theater. Cormac Theater had acquired a reputation for producing the best Shakespearean productions in the New World. It had a fine building, the best talent money could afford, and costumes that rivaled the finest theaters in England. Anne Cormac saw to that, too.

Unlike in her mother country—Ireland—in Charles Town, money could buy social position.

Chapter 1

The early evening air that encased Goose Creek Plantation was infused with the intoxicating perfume of gardenia blossoms. Like most late spring, summer, and early autumn days in coastal South Carolina, humidity spread a moist veil—like a shroud over literally everything—living and dead. This was especially true of the areas surrounded by the marsh. As a resident of Charles Town, you expected the all-pervasive shroud and the perfumes that permeated it, some not nearly so pleasant as the aroma of gardenias.

On the front porch, called the piazza by some and veranda by others (those Charles Town folks do have colorful ways about them), Anne Cormac sat with her granddaughter.

Anne had taken her father's surname after the death of her second husband (or was it her third? No matter). Cormac was a name she could keep regardless of her sleeping arrangements. Besides, her father's name was more suited to the owner of Goose Creek Plantation since he had enjoyed a positive reputation as an important lawyer and factor in the city. It was certainly more suited to her businesses and charitable, philanthropic endeavors than that of any of her buccaneering husbands' names.

Controversy had followed Anne throughout her entire life. It was something she had grown to expect even as a young girl. It had provided her with a full and interesting life.

On the eve of her 18th birthday, granddaughter Annie

(last name totally unimportant to this story) was seated, legs askew, on the porch swing across from her grandmother, for whom she was named, who was in her favorite rocking chair. Slowly swinging and slowly rocking together, they watched the effortless transition from evening into night. The young girl's frock lay in as undignified a manner as her legs, though it appeared to be of little concern to her. She was caught in that awkward season between girlhood and womanhood. She was there with her grandmother, and she was comfortable, and that was all that mattered.

The older woman glanced over at the swing to admire the beautiful young woman her granddaughter had become and noticed the unladylike position assumed by the teenager. The casual way she was sitting with her knees apart and her chemise bunched near her waist left her private parts open to view by anyone on the porch.

"Annie girl! Look after your frock. I am sittin' here looking right at your treasures!"

Being ladylike was as much a part of the older woman's complex character and personality as her low country Carolina accent. The flowery selection of descriptors from her Irish heritage added spice and texture to the grand background of Goose Creek Plantation, as did her insistence of dressing for dinner even when she was the only one dining.

"Granny Anne," the girl's frustration was evident in the inflection of her voice, "it's just you and me here, and I know you're not looking, so what difference does it make?"

"Annie, my dear girl, being a lady, a *Cormac* lady, makes all the difference. It is of the utmost importance especially in this day and time. Throughout your life, I've tried to teach you what I've had to learn the hard way. Being a lady means more than looking your best all of the time. It's how you think. It's being aware of yourself and your surroundings, even when you don't think anyone is watching. It's about *taking* advantage—and not *being* taken advantage of. How do you think I have succeeded as I have? So, remember to watch yourself and watch out *for* yourself. And pull your dress down, right now."

Anne's reproach of Annie's breech of Southern etiquette resulted in a stiff, uncomfortable silence that was broken only by the sounds of the evening. The heady aroma of the gardenia drew a broad smile across Anne's beautiful, though time-worn and well-traveled, face. She looked gentle, even frail, as she rocked softly in her rocking chair.

Annie shifted in the swing. As she fidgeted with her frock to cover her legs, and her treasures, Anne focused her attention intently on her only granddaughter.

"Sweet Annie," she said, "you look so beautiful tonight. What's left of the setting sun makes your fiery red hair and your complexion simply glow."

"Thank you, Granny Anne. Looking at you I can tell that beauty must be a part of our family legacy." The young girl was as much at home with her beauty as she was with the old porch swing and her grandmother.

There was another, less awkward silence, broken only when the older woman stood up and lighted the oil lanterns.

Annie watched the woman who had been like a mother to her, actually more than her mother. It was Anne's straight forward education that had prepared Annie to be ready for womanhood. Anne had clearly corrected the story of *the birds and the bees* into a realistic presentation of sexual relationships. It was Anne who prepared Annie and many of her friends to be ready for the monthly activity that separated women from men. Anne was responsible for so many things that Annie had learned that the girl could not imagine life without Granny Anne.

As Anne Cormac returned to the rocking chair, it was her pronouncement that broke the silence. "You know, Annie, all of this will be yours very soon. I'm almost 65 years old and I have lived a very adventurous life. Some say that I have robbed the death angel as many times as I robbed the ships of the English crown. In truth, I have lived well beyond my allotted time."

"Now you stop that kind of talk, Granny Anne. You've got lots of years left." The teenager knew her grandmother was speaking the truth, but the thought of being without her hurt much too deeply to imagine or to admit.

"Hush, my dear. I won't be with you too much longer, and that's the Lord's own truth." The silence that followed served to magnify the strange quality of the moment the two women shared and highlighted their unusual relationship.

"I want you to know that I have made all of the necessary arrangements for you to inherit Goose Creek Plantation. A substantial amount of money comes with it. I tell you this tonight because it is a part of my birthday gift to you. I have prepared you to take my place and tomorrow that will be made official. There is only one more thing I want to do for your birthday and that is to give you one gift that you want. Tell me what you want for your birthday . If it within my power to give, it is yours."

Annie thought for a few minutes before she spoke. "Granny Anne, before I ask for my special gift, may I ask you a question?"

"Why, certainly my dear."

Annie hesitated, selecting her words carefully. "I've heard so many stories about you and your life. Many seemed truly unbelievable. If what you say is true and you really only have a short time here, will you tell me about your life? The absolute truth?"

"Annie, me dear, dear girl," Anne's original Irish brogue slipped past the Charleston accent, almost as if another person was speaking. "I guess you would have heard a lot of stories about me. Yes, lots to be sure." Anne laughed softly before continuing. "Yes, I'll tell you the story of Anne Cormac. You deserve that. The real story. After all, it is as much a part of your birthright as your pretty face, those sparkling, emerald green eyes, your fiery red hair, this old house, and this sweet smelling land. I suspect most of what you have heard is probably true and then some. But, occasionally, I am surprised when I hear one of the tales of my exploits. You know how our 'low country' neighbors like to embellish a good story."

"Oh! Yes, yes," Annie's childlike excitement couldn't be contained by the ladylike body of the young woman sitting on the swing. She leaned forward, adjusting herself, pulling her knees up to her chest while making sure that she kept herself covered with her dress. Hugging her knees with her arms, she settled in for the beginning of the true-life story of Anne Bonny Cormac, the person she loved most in the entire world.

Yes, she had heard the stories of her grandmother's many lovers, her pirating years, her questionable birth, and the stories of her youth when she was certainly anything but ladylike.

Annie had always wondered if the stories could possible be true. They seemed so unlike the dignified pillar of society she knew as her grandmother. But Granny Anne had never openly talked about her past, and Annie feared to ask her about her life. Truth be told, Annie wasn't really sure she wanted to know if the stories were true or not. Those stories were, however, as much a part of her grandmother as the shroud of humidity that hung over Goose Creek Plantation and Charleston.

Now, at last, she would have the truth or at least as much truth as Granny Anne was willing to tell.

Chapter 2

"I was born in Ireland, in Kinsale, County Cork, in March of 1698. I have been told so many different dates that I selected March 8th to make it easier. I can't remember why I chose March 8th. I must have had a good reason." The old woman pondered for a moment before continuing.

"My father, your great grandfather, was a very prominent Irish barrister. My mother was a servant, actually a maid, employed by my father to look after his house, attend to his family, and his wife. This is the story surrounding my birth as I was told it by my father, and the one I believe. My father's wife came down with an illness that was prevalent in the city. Their physician advised her to leave the city for a change of air. It was agreed that she should sojourn for a time at my father's mother's house, a half-days travel from the family mansion.

"During the separation, my father became infatuated with the maid and a full blown affair developed. In the beginning, keeping the affair from his wife wasn't too difficult, since she wasn't living in the house. She was none the wiser. You must understand, William Cormac and his wife were a proper Catholic family. For the affair to be made public would be much more than merely embarrassing—it would be a total social and financial disaster. But when the maid, Mary Brennan was her name, turned up pregnant, the situation changed entirely.

"Back in the Old Country, it was not an uncommon occurrence for a servant girl to turn up pregnant. Even if the Master of the Manor was the father, the servant girl would usually just be returned to her parents, and some financial arrangement made for the girl's family to remain silent. But Mary was an orphan, so that wasn't a option. William Cormac was faced with a hard choice. He could turn the servant girl out into the streets to fend for herself, or deal with the situation head on regardless of the outcome.

"My father told me that he was inextricably in love with my mother, and in his words, 'life without her would not be worth a single breath.' So you see, Annie girl, our birthright, in fact our destiny is to be great lovers.

"Divorce was certainly a possibility. All it required was the Arch Bishop's concurrence with a parish priest. It was only an issue of the right amount of money. But my father knew that the divorce and the pregnancy would be too much for the small Irish parish to handle, especially if all of the players were still on the scene. He knew that the stigma would follow him and my mother and me, not to mention his wife, who was not at any fault, for our entire lives and for generations to come. A normal life would be impossible for any of us. He also realized that in order to stay with his true love, he would have to leave his wife, his home, and his homeland.

"From my own memories of my mother and from what my father told me of her, my mother was a beautiful woman. She looked much like you, dear Annie, with silky, shiny red hair that fell in cascades of curls from the top of her head to her slim waist. Her complexion was as smooth as a well-polished river rock. Her eyes were emerald green, as deep an emerald green as the ocean that laps the shore of the Emerald Isle itself. But, when she was angry, yellow sparks would flare in those the deep emerald green eyes igniting them into a fiery hazel. Make no doubt about it; everyone around Miss Mary knew when they had crossed over her line."

There was a moment of silence. Then Anne continued with her story of her father and the love of his life, Mary Brennan.

"Following his heart, he chose divorce. The affair was made public by his wife when she found out about the divorce. It was a short time after I was born, I'm told. My father packed some of his law books and personal effects, mostly clothes and some family valuables. My mother had few clothes. With all of their belongings packed and what money my father could get his hands on, my father and mother boarded a ship with their one-year-old baby girl and headed for Charles Town in 1699. He told me that the only ship that they could afford passage on was a slow sailing vessel that took eight weeks to get to Charles Town, our new home.

"We missed the earthquake in 1699 and the subsequent fire that destroyed a third of the town. When we arrived the rebuilding had already started, but living arrangements for a new family were meager. At first we lived in one room that was owned by the Anabaptist church.

"My father was an affable, intelligent, and convivial person, and he was a hard worker. Reverend Samuel Thomas, the pastor of the Anabaptist church took a liking to my father and helped him find work. It didn't take long for him to gain steady employment with one of the factors since he knew English law and was a competent attorney. With better employment he soon found finer accommodations for us to abide in.

"Mary was presented as my father's wife and I as his

daughter. No one seemed to question either. By 1704, my father was employed by Colonel William Rhett to manage all of his business holdings including his plantation, his financial concerns— his cotton brokering, his shipping business, and his dock facility. All of the businesses flourished under my dad's management. For that, he was well paid.

"A year later, the owner of Goose Creek Plantation had money problems and my father, with Colonel Rhett's help, was able to buy the plantation. It was a very happy day when my mother, my father, and I moved into this very house. Of course, it was much smaller then, but it was a major step up for us. We moved into the house with all of its furnishings. I had my own room. Our family was accepted and included in Charles Town society and its social events. Those, I think, were the happiest days of my life."

Anne paused as traces of long forgotten memories flitted through her mind. Annie noticed a strange smile tiptoe across her grandmother's face.

"What are you thinking about, Granny Anne?"

"Nothing, really," Anne answered but the younger woman knew that a thought had somehow brought the older woman pleasure.

"I had started primary school by then and I'm told I was quite a handful for my mother, my teacher, and everyone else—except my father.

"I experienced one of the worst times in my life in 1706. My mother contracted the Fever—what we now know as Yellow Fever. She died within a few weeks. She is buried here on the plantation, but you already know that. A major part of my life was taken away from me, and I blamed everyone in Charles Town for her death.

"Initially, I turned my anger and grief into energy, helping my father on the plantation. He taught me everything I would need to know when I took over the plantation. I was a quick study and he was a good teacher. We spent many hours together. He also taught me to ride, which is why I was such a good horsewoman. He was a fencer when he was in college and he was very good. He started teaching me to fence, and later to use a sword, and it didn't take long for me to become better than he was. That skill has served me well. I guess he had wanted another child, a son, so I'm sure that's why I was such a *tomboy*. Also, I'm sure I was trying to take my mother's place in his life. Although he seemed happy with me and my help, I knew there was a hole in his life that no one would ever fill.

"I have said I was a handful, which was to true. I listened to no one except my father. I had grown tall, and working along side my father on the plantation combined with my fencing classes had made me strong and agile. I was a strong, scrapping 10-year-old girl with a very bad attitude. Oh, and before you ask, ladylike was not in my life. One of the smart-ass older boys in the school started trying to bully me and one of the other girls. There was a fight. I beat him rather badly. He left school that day with a black eye, a bloodied nose, a cut lip, and what they thought might be a broken arm. I heard later that he had some internal injuries. It was two weeks before he returned to school. I was disciplined, but he didn't mess with me anymore and neither did any of the other boys."

That strange smile was back on the older woman's face. Anne settled deep in her rocking chair as she paused in her voyage down the rivers of the past. The uneasy silence caused Annie to have concerns about her grandmother. She shifted her position on the swing and stared hard at Anne. She wanted to make sure her grandmother hadn't given up the ghost. It was an other-worldly sigh that signaled the reuniting of the older Anne's spirit with her body.

"Are you alright, Granny Anne?" Leaning a little too far forward on the swing caused Annie to slip from the swing and land hard on her bottom. Her yelp was more from surprise than physical harm. She quickly regained her feet, straightened her frock, and settled back onto the swing, before both women started laughing.

"Sweet Annie," there was a distance in Anne's voice and it sounded weaker. "Let's continue this conversation tomorrow. I am really not feeling well."

The two walked into the house side by side, climbed the stairs together, then separated and went to their individual bedrooms on the second floor of the plantation house.

Truth be told, reliving the memories from her girlhood had overwhelmed the older woman. It was suddenly clear to her that no matter how strong she had been throughout her life, there were things in her life she didn't want to relive.

The moonlight flooding her bedroom window was especially bright on that warm autumn night. Cotton, grown by her slaves and woven into soft sheets by her servants, caressed her weary body. Anne Cormac had long since taken to sleeping in the nude, especially on the warm summer nights, because she valued comfort over convention. The attendant controversy she considered an added benefit. Anne Cormac knew that, thanks to the underground communications network that existed among the servants and slaves on the low country plantations, she would be the subject of conversation among the *proper* ladies. They talked about everything, but the unconventional got even more attention.

That same network had been an effective means for her to learn a great deal of information that had served her well in the management and profitability of her plantation, as well as in her other, less legal endeavors. She knew when other plantation owners were having money problems. She knew when they were especially vulnerable, and she knew when ships carrying especially large shipments of gold and other treasures were expected. That information was particularly helpful when Anne decided to, occasionally, dabble in her earlier career—piracy— though due to her advancing years she had not conducted an *adventure*, as she called it, in over a decade.

The singing from the slave quarters died out, as did their fires. The only sound was the croaking of the bullfrogs vying for attention. Their croaking was the music to which sleep danced a two-step into Anne's bedchambers that night.

Chapter 3

Sleep, when it came was fitful for Anne Cormac. Her dreams were filled with specters of the past. First came the faces, many that she had pushed deep into her subconscious. Some were victims of her superb swordsmanship, her strength and her agility. Many were her sexual conquests, best described as the good, the bad, and the ugly. There were buccaneers—some famous, others infamous—and the ne'er-do-wells that crewed for them.

There were places in her dreams as well. *Groggerie* where the seamen found their three Ws—*whiskey, wenches, and widdles.* The small rooms that doubled as brothels. The filthy ships and the dirty towns that they called ports.

And the prisons.

The visions played out on the stage of her mind; many long since forgotten, and many she wished had remained buried like cursed plunder. But in that sleep state, that altered-consciousness where reality and perception, remembered and forgotten, real and imagined blend, Anne Cormac wrestled with the moment, and with what she should—and what she would—divulge to her granddaughter.

The beginnings of dawn brought Anne back to the conscious world. The sounds of the slaves beginning their workday. The animal sounds from the barn. The crowing rooster. And the stirring in the house as servants prepared for the start of another day. Breakfast would soon be ready. She slipped into a silk robe and walked to her granddaughter's room. Annie was already up, dressed, and sitting on the side of the bed, which was quite unusual for the teenager.

"Good Morning, Sweet Annie. It's good to see you already up," the surprise in her voice was something she couldn't hide. "Ready for the morning duties?"

"I certainly am, Granny Anne," the young woman answered. "But more ready to get back to the story you will be telling me."

"There is much about the plantation that needs tending to," Anne stated. She needed some more time to decide exactly what she was going to tell her granddaughter. "My story can wait till after dinner."

The two split up and went about their assigned chores. Annie got the grain bucket, filled it with freshly ground corn and headed to the chicken yard. Anne gave instructions to the kitchen servants then headed for the horse barn. William, the lead slave in charge of the horses, was in the barn attending Anne's favorite horse who was expected to foal anytime. Anne sent for Annie as soon as she realized the immediacy of the event. Annie arrived as the little filly came into the world. Births were celebrated at Goose Creek Plantation whether human or animal, so this was a happy beginning to the day.

Suddenly pensive, Anne thought, *Another first step in the circle of life.* Aloud she said, "Sweet Annie, let's go to the Plantation House for noon meal. I'll need your help with the plantation books after we eat."

When the older woman addressed her granddaughter, it was always *Sweet Annie.* Annie had suggested that just her name was sufficient but, for Anne, *Sweet Annie* was second nature.

With the midday meal completed, Anne brought out the

books where she kept track of the costs and income of the plantation. It was her close attention to the numbers that resulted in continual profits at Goose Creek Plantation. Other Carolina plantations experienced up and down profits, with aristocratic owners who paid little attention to the details. Anne kept a close control on all expenses, so the good years were better and the lean years less painful than her more profligate neighbors. Many of the additions to her holdings were the direct result of owners who paid too little attention to the details of their estates. Anne Cormac learned at her father's elbow that if one penny slipped through the books, others would follow. It was a lesson she was determined that Annie would learn as well.

Anne and Annie met in the formal dining room. Anne insisted on dressing for the evening meal and both were dressed in fine dresses. There was a glass of wine set at each plate, a symbol of cultured elegance and dignity—and a sign that Annie was coming of age.

There was a happy atmosphere in the dining room. The foal was healthy and a welcome addition to the plantation's stock of fine thoroughbreds. All of the numbers had checked out and the plantation was profitable. Conversation was light and Annie was almost gleeful at the expectation of revisiting the life story of her notorious grandmother.

Anne was more subdued, and somewhat apprehensive about telling the next chapter in her life story. *You can't put the genie back in the bottle*, she mused. *You started it. Regardless of where the chips may fall, Annie deserves the truth.*

With the wine working its magic, the two moved together

to the veranda, and assumed their familiar places—one swinging, eyes bright in anticipation; one gently rocking, eyes closed, lips pursed in apprehension.

Anne started the next chapter of her tale with an apology of sorts.

"Sweet Annie, I am not proud of the next part of my life. But as we agreed, there'll be no sugar coating."

The old woman fixed her granddaughter with a stare, which Annie met with a quiet strength and dignity Anne had not noticed before. A smile crept across her lips and she nodded.

"Very well. I told you my mother had died and I blamed everyone for her death. I was a 10-year-old girl just beginning to have an appreciation of what it took for my mother to be where she was and where we were. And then she was gone. We were just beginning to build a relationship. And she was dead. The worst thing was, no one could tell me why. My closest friend was dead and the next closest friend couldn't tell me why. It was years later before my father could tell me that he was going through the same feelings as I was. So, I was blaming him as well.

"It all came to a head one night before the evening meal. I was going to sit where my mother sat at the table—some sort of statement that I was now the woman of the house, I suppose. Now remember I was a strong, scrapping 10-year-old with a bad attitude and a fierce temper, grieving the loss of my mother. I had moved my plate to my mother's place. A young scullery maid moved it back to what had been my place at the table. That became the focus and the culmination of all of my anger at my loss. I screamed at her and grabbed a carving knife from the table and buried it in her chest.

"Oh, it caused quite a commotion. I was still screaming at

her lifeless body, my father was screaming at me, and the rest of the servants were just screaming. My father was the first to get hold of his emotions and confirmed the girl was dead. He got the head servant to take care of the dead girl, calmed the rest of the servants, and took me out to this very porch. I truly don't remember what he said, but soon we were holding each other and we both were sobbing. That one action, that one moment, separated the woman I would become from the girl I left behind.

"My father was able pay off the girl's family and the chief constable. I was never arrested. The result was that the first droplet fell from my eye into what became the gulf that would separate my father and me for many years.

"I continued to help my father for the next four years but the passion was gone. I still worked at his elbow, but now it was just—work. I completed school that year, but I just didn't care about anything. One year rolled into the next. Finally I stopped working for the plantation. I stopped wanting to be with my father. I resented him. I resented the change that had taken place in him—and in me for that matter.

"When I came of marriageable age he would invite eligible young men to the plantation for me to meet. He wanted me to find one of them to marry and settle down. None of those local boys were even the slightest bit interesting to me. It was like they were a copy of each other, all snobbery and self-impressed. And they were just the sort of aristocratic foppery my father approved of.

"Charleston's population had grown to nearly 9,000 people, fewer than half were free and white, including the pirate community of around 250 although their numbers would rise and fall with the tide. The rest were slaves.

"I was now 15 years old. I was a woman in my mind and I had the breasts to prove it. One evening—I really don't remember why, bored I guess—I rode my horse into Charles Town to see what was happening. I suppose I was looking for some excitement to fill the holes in my life. I rode past the *1/2 Moon*, a notorious pirate hangout. There was loud music. There was loud talking. There was loud laughing. So I went in.

"That was the night of many firsts for me. I met a bunch of real pirates. I learned a new language—pirate talk. I had my first cup of *grog*. My first time to go *pogy*—that's *drunk* in pirate talk. I had my time *quaffing*—my first sexual experience, my first hangover, and my first night of sleeping on the floor in a filthy room. But even later, when I was *casting up accounts*—vomiting, I realized that during that evening of excitement, I was at last able to forget my anger and frustration. For the first time I was free of the disappointment I had carried since my mother's death.

"The pirates I met were free of pretension. I quickly learned that if there was more grabbing on my breast than I wanted, all I had to do was punch the offender in the stomach and kick them in their *nutmegs*. And, once I had collected a few *nutmegs,* word got around that I would retaliate, I was pretty much left alone. It was a lot like respect.

"Most pirates were older men, at least they appeared so to me, and they spent a lot of time drinking in the *groggeries*, so they weren't particularly appealing. It wasn't like I was one of them, nor was I a *three penny upright*—a wench who would have sex standing up for three pennies.

"As time passed, it was not unusual to see me at the 1/2 Moon, or *The Pink House,* or any of the numerous other *groggeries* that catered to the buccaneers that considered Charles

Town their home port. I got to the point that I loved what I believed to be the carefree life of a pirate. I was accepted by them. And then I met James Bonny. Thus began the next chapter of my life.

"But that's another story. We can talk about that tomorrow night. Now, to bed my Sweet Annie."

Chapter 4

The morning chores seemed to drag by for Annie, yet the time moved much too fast for Anne. She still didn't know how much of her saga she would tell Annie, though she had promised the whole truth.

They finished the day's responsibilities and rechecked the numbers for the plantation's book. That really wasn't necessary, but Anne wanted an excuse to delay the telling of the next chapter in her life. With the evening meal completed, the servants cleared the table and the Cormac ladies settled themselves in their now accustomed positions.

"Let's see. Where was I when I stopped yesterday," Anne said almost to herself, but she actually voiced that thought loud enough for Annie to overhear.

"You were about to tell me about James Bonny, how you met him, and what the two of you did. Did you really burn the plantation house when you left?" Annie was quick to start the evening's story time.

"Hold your horses, Sweet Annie. There is a lot that happened before that—and don't believe everything you hear about me and when I left Charles Town."

Anne had asked a kitchen servant to bring tea for her and Annie. It arrived shortly after the two had gotten comfortable. Anne stirred the lumps of sugar into the hot cup of tea and squeezed a slice of lemon. Annie followed suit. Anne sipped at her cup. She cleared her throat and started the story.

"Remember, I was 15 years old. Almost every evening you could find me at The Pink House or the 1/2 Moon with my new friends—a group of crusty, dirty, rowdy, old pirates. They were my peers and I enjoyed a reputation of being a fierce fighter with a fiery temper and a vicious disposition. Believe me, I had no interest in any of them, however they were the perfect diversion for my depressed, wounded ego. There was always excitement in these *groggeries*. And, as I said, I enjoyed a degree of respect from these men—at least from my point of view I was close to being equal. At home, I did my duties, I ran the plantation with the help of the chief steward who had been with my father since before he purchased the plantation. He always asked for my involvement, but I was certain he could manage without my help or management skills. Almost everything was perfect.

"Then, one evening, *he* walked into The Pink House. He was the youngest person there by a number of years, except me, of course. He was a good five inches taller than me. He had wavy brown hair. He was clean-shaven. He wasn't like any of the other pirates in the room, but no one but a pirate would be seen in The Pink House. He walked to the bar without speaking to any of the other pirates. He didn't talk to any of the three penny uprights. He just ordered a whisky. One of the wenches who was *sporting her dairy* .—showing off her breasts, walked up to him and whispered in his ear. He said no and pushed her aside. I asked one of my pirate friends who he was. I was told he was James Bonny and that he was new. 'If a wagging tongue were money he would be worth a million gold pieces,' the fellow laughed.

"I didn't laugh, but I did smile. I sauntered my way over to him and asked him his name direct. He looked at me with his crystal blue eyes. 'I'm Captain James Bonny,' he breathed. Well, my heart melted. I had never felt like that before. I remember thinking, *A real live pirate captain.*

"He wasn't like the rest of the rabble in the bar—crusty, dirty, rowdy, old. And he wasn't like the men my father had introduced me to when he was trying to match me up—those boring, weak, snooty, simple-minded, pushy young men in Charles Town's society. He was definitely different.

"We talked about nothing for the rest of the evening. I wanted to be next to him. I wanted to be a pirate on his boat. I even remember thinking that I would like to bear his children. I thought I knew the ins and outs of being a woman, but these were new thoughts for me. I waited for him to suggest we go quaffing in one of the nearby brothel rooms. To my surprise he said he had to leave but he would be back tomorrow night. And with that pronouncement, he left. I didn't know if I were dreaming or what. But I did know he was different from every man I had ever met.

"Shortly after his departure, I fetched my horse and rode home. I thought about him all of the way home. He would have been the man of my dreams—if I had ever dreamed about a man. I couldn't sleep. I kept seeing those eyes.

"The next evening, I was back at The Pink House. He arrived much as he had the night before. We talked again, this time, at the end of the evening, we agreed to meet again the next day at midday at the same place. And we did. The Pink House seemed different during the day; quiet and void of excitement. But Captain James Bonny was there. As we walked to the *Palisades* he told me of his ship that had been taken from him. He talked about his treasures as we passed the AnaBaptist Church, the English Church and as we stopped at the drawbridge at the Town Line he kissed me. It was a soft, tender kiss, not at all the way the old pirates kissed the wenches at The Pink House or the 1/2 Moon. We continued our walk as he told me of the ports where he had docked and his exploits at sea. He said he wanted to spend time with me, that he was interested in me. We passed the *Colleton Bastion*, the *Court of Guards*, and the 1/2 Moon.

"By that time The Pink House was open and we had a grog and he continued to talk. When it got too noisy we went outside. He offered to *crack Jenny's tea cup*—a pirate expression to have sex—and even that sounded caring. So we moved into one of the brothel rooms where we spent the rest of the night talking and having sex.

"I rode home the next morning thinking I had met the perfect man for me. He was sophisticated, but not like those *boys* my father introduced me to. He was a man of the world, a pirate captain, so he was exciting like my new friends. While we were reviewing the plantation books, I told my father about my day with my new pirate captain friend. My father asked his name and I proudly said, 'Captain James Bonny.' Little did I know that my father would check him out. There is no way a person could be as successful as my father without making some powerful friends. My father's only advice was to be careful.

"I had agreed to meet Captain James—that's what I called him—at sundown at The Pink House. I arrived before him. I asked the barkeep if Captain James had been in. He said 'Who?' I said, you know, he was here last night—Captain James Bonny. He said, 'Oh, Bonny,' then he looked at me with an almost fatherly expression and asked, 'Do you remember that I said, if a wagging tongue were money he would be worth a million gold pieces? Be careful girl. Just be careful.'

"I heard him talking, but his words never made it past my ears.

"About that time Captain James entered The Pink House and he was walking toward me. He ordered us grogs and we moved to a table. We finished our drinks then walked outside. It was a warm summer evening, not unlike tonight, Sweet Annie. He suggested that we go to one of the brothel rooms. We had sex again and he told me that he had gotten word that there was a rich English ship expected in Charles Town sometime the next month. He was going to intercept it, he said, and he would have a lot of money. He said he would be gone as much as a month and he would let me know when he returned. There was a moment of silence—and then he asked if I would like to sail with him sometime.

"I hadn't considered that possibility until he mouthed the words. He knew that I was a fierce fighter. I had told him that my father had taught me to fence and that I was already better than my teacher. Just the thought of being a real pirate was exciting enough, but the idea of going to battle next to the man that I was infatuated with was overwhelming.

"I remember saying—'Yes, yes, yes!'

"For the first time we really made love. It was slow, passionate, meaningful. Months later I would find that it was only meaningful to me.

"When we finished, James told me that he would be sailing at high tide the next afternoon. He asked me to meet him the next morning.

"Sleep that night was intermittent at best. Dreams were visions of being a pirate; of me standing next to Captain James on the quarterdeck of a *trimaster*, of sifting through chests of golden coins. Truth be told, it was rare for a ship to be carrying gold, but those were my dreams. Actually, more than my greatest expectation. And, in my dreams, it was within my grasp.

"I was up early, saddled, and on my way to The Pink House. It wasn't long after I arrived that Captain James appeared. He had walked to The Pink House from what I assumed was his schooner moored at the dock not far from where we were. He handed me a rolled rug. I unrolled it and there was a cutlass and a rapier and two flintlock pistols.

"'I want you to practice with the cutlass and the rapier. They will be your primary weapons. The cutlass is heaver than the epee you used to fence with. The rapier is lightweight and should be a good weapon for you. You are strong, but your agility will be your best weapon in a sword fight. I will get you a couple of daggers for close fighting,' he said. It was important that he was treating me as an adult, not a child.

"'Practice. Learn to adapt your fencing moves to both the cutlass and the rapier. You will be unbeatable.'

"We kissed passionately. He stepped back and said one word as he turned to head for his ship—'Practice!'

"I didn't know whether to cry, laugh, shout, or smile as he walked away. In the end, I smiled as I rolled the weapons back up in the rug-like container. I got on my horse and rode at a slow plod back toward the plantation. That smile never left my face.

"I passed my father on the way. He was riding to his office. I am sure he saw the roll that contained the weapons hanging from my saddle, but he didn't mention it. He had only one question—'Will you be at the plantation house for evening meal tonight?' I assured him that I would, and we parted heading in different directions. When I got home, I handed the bridle to William, the servant that handled the horses, and carefully carried the roll that secreted my treasures up to my room and placed it among my personal stuff.

"I set to work on the plantation books, but I could not concentrate. My mind kept wandering to the quarterdeck of a sleek sailing ship with me standing at the side of Captain James Bonny.

"My father arrived home only a few minutes before the evening meal. We ate in silence. Once he finished his last bite, he pushed back from the table and stared at me for a long moment. Then he said, 'Daughter.'

"He never called me *Daughter* unless he was angry, or if what he had to say was of particular importance. He repeated that name. 'Daughter,' he said. 'We need to talk about your new friend, James Bonny.'

"I interrupted him, 'You mean *Captain* James Bonny.'

"'No, I mean James Bonny. First of all, he's not a captain. He is a sometime pirate and from what I have heard, not a very good one, at that. I think it would be best if you stop seeing him.'

"My father, who I loved more than anything, had crossed a line and stepped into an area that made me furious. I remember that evening like it was yesterday. Realize that it was almost 50 years ago, but I still remember every word, every gesture, every emotion like it was yesterday. I screamed at him, 'You don't want me to be happy. Not since my mother died. You brought us to this evil place and that's why she died. It's your fault. You don't care about me. All you care about is your business and this place.' And I stormed out of the room. I came out to this very porch and sat in that very swing, right where you are sitting. I was sobbing my heart out.

"My father followed me out and sat next to me. He tried to console me. I remember he said, 'Daughter, you know I love you with all my heart. This *place,* as you call it, is your future. It will be yours someday. *Captain* Bonny, as you call him, is just trying to get you to fall in love with him so that he can marry you and get control of our plantation. He's a charlatan and a loser.'

"Those words are what separated me from my father for the next 10 years. I quit sobbing, lifted my chin high, and left him sitting on the swing. I marched to my room. From that moment there was a unsurpassable gulf between us. I felt it. I'm sure that he did too.

"Oh, I continued to keep the plantation books, and I would occasionally go to The Pink House, mostly to inquire about Captain Bonny. But the excitement was gone.

"My only enjoyment at that time was practicing my sword work. There wasn't a tree on the plantation that went unchallenged. They all felt the sting of my cutlass and my rapier. My father had stopped talking James down, but the only reason for my *making up* with him, was to continue my fencing lessons. He was amazed at how good I had become. He didn't realize my skill and determination were fueled by my anger. He began to teach me defensive moves, which when combined with my natural agility made me unbeatable, even though he was a gifted and practiced fencer. I continued to practice, too.

"One evening I asked him if he would teach me to shoot. I knew he had pistols very similar to the ones James had given me. So one afternoon we took his pistols out on the farm and he showed me how to shoot and reload. I was accomplished at shooting in the same way I was at fencing. I suppose natural skills run in the family.

"My father taught me that the real skill of using a pistol was the speed of reloading. I spend many hours in my room at night practicing reloading my pistols. I even developed some short cuts that allowed me to reload very fast.

"I was doing exactly what James told me to do, and I was getting very good at it.

"Then, one night I decided to go to The Pink House. The barkeep or *Tapster* told me that James was back from his adventure. I waited until he arrived at The Pink House. We spent a passionate evening together, and the next day we met again at the Palisades. He told me of all of his escapades and he said that he had sent the sloop on to New Province in the Bahamas. I knew from my buccaneering friends that New Providence and the Nassau Harbor was called the Republic of Pirate. He talked about taking up where we left off. I told him of my confrontation with my father and that I was ready to be Mrs. Captain James Bonny. I took his hesitation to be from my surprise pronouncement. But he said that was a good idea, so we agreed we would meet at the *Court of Guard* to register for marriage.

"I rode home to gather some clothes and my weapons and announce my intention to my father. He was furious. He forbade me to get married, but in South Carolina at that time, it was legal to get married when you were 10 years old, so he had no legal grounds to prevent me. I'm sure he knew that. He again said that James Bonny was only after the plantation and his money, and he again said that James was no ship's captain. I told him that I didn't care. He ended the conversation by saying if we were married, he would disown me so *my Captain James Bonny* would never get his plantation nor his money. I told him I didn't care and I was certain that *my Captain James Bonny* wouldn't care either. With that, I left the table and went to my room.

"I left the plantation early the next morning. I didn't want to continue the argument with my father. Captain James and I met at the *Court of Guards* and we were married. That was the beginning of two years of disappointments.

"Sweet Annie, I am tired and this is a good place to stop."

The old woman examined the sad countenance on her granddaughter's face, nodded, then went up the stairs to her bedroom.

Chapter 5

Anne opened a window before getting ready for bed. The smells of home flowed in her bedroom floating on the comfortable coolness of evening. The sweet smell of the gardenia blossoms, the familiar smells of the marsh—these were the night smells of home.

She sat by the window looking out at the plantation illuminated by a gibbous moon and considered her life. Agreeing to tell Annie her true story had dredged up long-forgotten memories—some happy; others less so. The moonlight cast dancing shadows. It was a night not unlike the night of her first real pirate battle.

There had been a full moon. The freighter had dozens of oil lamps burning, giving the ship an almost festive appearance. The pirate sloop sailed dark to be unseen. The light from all of the lamps made the ship an easy target. They had already thrown the grappling hooks before anyone on the freighter knew they were there. Three of the hooks bit deep, and the ship was quickly pulled and connected to the pirate ship. There was a fierce bump when the ships contacted each other, knocking many of the freighter's crew to the deck. The boarding crew were ready and stormed aboard the freighter. It took precious minutes for the watch to regain their footing and sound the alarm. By that time the pirate boarding team was at full strength.

Sitting there by the window Anne relived that unforgettable

night—the night the first man was to experience the skill of her swordsmanship in battle. He was much taller than she, and more muscular. He carried a broad sword, much heaver than her rapier, so she knew he would be slower. She gave him the first swing. He smiled, under the delusion that superior strength and size gave him the advantage. Anne simply dodged his first swing.

He reset and took a mightier swing, thinking that a more powerful delivery would end her. Now it was Anne's turn to smile. She realized that her fencing and practiced sword skills gave her the advantage in any sword fight.

The second swing of his broad sword went wide of his target as she simply moved to her right. The weight of his sword carried his body to his right exposing his left side, and she plunged her rapier into his heart. The look of shock and surprise was the image of his death mask as he crumpled to his knees.

Anne watched for a moment, then withdrew her rapier from the lifeless body. She wiped his blood from the blade on his waistcoat and moved on to the next fight. She heard the wooosh as a sword that just missed her head. She snatched out her pistol and fired. The force of the blast took off the seaman's head and sent it rolling haphazardly down the ship's deck as his body did a death dance at her feet.

Anne ducked and turned, pulling her other pistol in time to see a sailor running toward her with dagger drawn. She fired. Time slowed, and she watched as the lead ball flew from the muzzle, hitting him in mid-chest with such force that it stopped his forward motion. It took a few moments before he drew his last ragged breath. His arm, still holding the dagger in a death grip, dropped and the blade buried itself into his thigh.

With the skill of many hours of practice, she reloaded both pistols and began the search for the next victim. No one was in sight. Then she heard the call of the captain to "Stand down." The battle was over.

With those words echoing in her ears, Anne returned to the present. She realized she was soaked in sweat. She picked up a petticoat she had removed earlier that evening and mopped off the sweat. The combination of the long-forgotten memory, the cool night air, and her damp body caused a chill that left her skin covered in goosebumps. That event was certainly a part of her life, but the memory was one she had long since placed in a locked room in her heart. She devoutly wished it would remain forgotten.

There was silence in the plantation house, broken only by the night marsh sounds. She had no idea what time it was, but the slave quarters were quiet so it must be late.

She slipped between the fine cotton sheets. As she lay in her comfortable bed, her mind kept taking her to many past nights she spent in uncomfortable surroundings. The dirty, smelly ship's sleeping spaces; the dirty, smelly hovels where she had lived; the dirty, smelly prisons—all memories she thought were locked in that secret room forever. Her talks with Annie were the key that unlocked that room, and the memories would not be contained.

The rest of the night might have been filled with dream— the faces of victims, the spoils of pirating, the salt spray of the sea, and the cries of the dead and dying. But the dreams fled with the rising of the sun. Morning arrived at the plantation, and all things continued as if nothing had changed at all.

This was a big day in Charles Town. It was opening day for the very successful Drury Lane production of King John.

It was one of Shakespeare's most successful plays in London and now it was opening at the Cormac Theater in Charles Town. The play listed 28 characters. Anne had paid to transport 14 of the original actors including David Garrick as King John, Colley Cibber as Constance, and T. Sheridan as Phillip the Bastard, and all of the costumes and sets to her theater. The lesser characters were to be played by actors from New York.

Storytelling would be interrupted that evening by the theater event. Anne insisted that all chores be done before she and Annie could make the trip to Charles Town. It was a special performance. A number of people had traveled for days to be present. All available rooms at Charles Town inns were rented and many people stayed with friends. Anne had decided that she and Annie would make a grand entrance, but in her own unique way. She had employed the costume designer for the theater to design special dresses for the pair. They would arrive on horseback. Their gowns were made in pieces and attached to appear as if it were a single grand gown. The skirt and train were attached to the top and on the sides of their riding pants. The front was split in the center and could be attached across the front with discrete hooks, allowing them to wear jodhpurs to facilitate riding. The train rolled up and looked like a bustle on the back.

Arrive in style, they did. The ladies of Goose Creek Plantation rode in on a matched pair of white stallions. They were met by the show's dressers, and thanks to Anne's unique dress design, the pair were quickly transformed into the most stylish show-goers. The Royal Governor opened the evening and proclaimed that Charles Town was the fourth-biggest port in the new world with only Philadelphia, Boston, and

New York being larger. Thanks to Charles Town's position in trade, the town was the largest and wealthiest in the South with a population of 11,000. In addition to his insightful management, he credited successful professionals such as Anne Cormac and her father for the position Charles Town enjoyed. The play was a rousing success. Anne and Annie were the most gracious, ladylike hosts for the production and the reception that followed.

More than once during the festivities Anne was struck by Annie's appearance. She was her own mirrored image. She was Anne Cormac in her finery. It triggered another memory—the image of Anne Bonny, the fierce, bloodthirsty pirate dressed in men's clothing. Even now she was amazed that the two nearly opposite women could inhabit the same body.

At the end of the evening Anne and Annie met at their mounts and as the dressers prepared the pair for their ride home Annie said, "This was such a wonderful evening, Granny Anne. But I can't wait to get back to your story."

"Soon enough, Sweet Annie, soon enough."

During much of the next day, the plantation chores were interrupted by dozens of well-wishers, many on their way back to their homes throughout the Carolinas.

Anne begged off story time that evening. She was tired and it had been a busy couple of days. She assured Annie that she would pick up where she left off the next evening.

In her bedroom, Anne Cormac again sat gazing out her window view of the plantation, at lease what she could see of it. Clouds obscured the stars and there was very little moonlight. Embers from the fires in the slave quarters produced an occasional flare as they died out. The usual sounds were there. The sounds of home.

As she slipped between the sheets she said a short prayer. "God please let me have a good, dreamless night's sleep."

God, it seems, did not answer her prayer.

Sleep was filled with more dreams. The dirty *groggeries*, the stinking ships, and the filthy room in New Providence that the lying James Bonny found for them to live.

For two nights now, her mind was making her relive her buccaneering days so she wouldn't forget even the smallest detail as she told her life story to her Sweet Annie. There was much she was not proud of, but they were part of the story.

Soon enough the bad dreams were replaced by peaceful sleep; sleep that was interrupted far too soon by the sounds of morning.

Chapter 6

Annie had arose, beating her grandmother at getting up. That was a major change from having to wake her and motivate her morning movement. They had a quick cup of coffee and cheese biscuit made by the cook, then commenced morning chores.

They checked on the new foal—he was up, alert, and frisky and would soon join the other horses—before moving through their morning routine. They took a break for lunch, did the bookwork, and oversaw a multitude of other tasks common to the running of the plantation before adjourning to the porch for mid-afternoon tea, a custom Anne carried with her from England. Settled and comfortable, Anne continued her story.

"Let's see, Sweet Annie. I told you that my relationship with my Captain James Bonny had caused a massive argument with my father. He told me that he had investigated my *captain* and found him to be an impostor and a liar. That was the most angry I had ever been with my father. I cried angry tears and those tears added to the gulf that had separated us.

"You remember, I went to the *Court of Guard* with James the next morning and we were married. We went to my father's office and announced the news. My father was quite calm—I'm sure he knew what was going to happen and he also knew there was little he could do to stop me. I also believe he knew some of what the future held for me. He asked James only one question—about one of ships James had described in detail to me, and that I had described to my father. The story James recounted to my father was quite different from what he had told me. My father didn't challenge him but when he was finished, my father looked directly at me and asked me one question; 'Do you remember what I said I would do if you went through with this?'

"I was livid. The anger from the loss of my mother, the blame I had leveled at my father, and the lack of his trust concerning my marriage to Captain James Bonny boiled to the surface. I slammed my fist on his desk and screamed at him, 'Keep your precious plantation. You love it more than you love me. James and I will be just fine without your money.' With that, I grabbed James' arm and we left the office. I jumped on my horse, told James to get on behind me and we road to the plantation. On the way James asked what my father had meant by his question. I told him, 'My father said if I married you, he would disown me.' James said he was certain he didn't mean that. 'You obviously didn't know my father,' I snapped back. 'He's probably drawing up the papers as we're riding away.'

"I know you have heard a story that before I left for New Providence, I burned this house to the ground. That isn't true. It was the barn I set on fire. I was told later that much of it did burn and it had to be rebuilt, but the slaves and the servants were able to get the animals out. For that I am grateful. The animals never did me any harm.

"On the ride back into town, I asked James where his ship was moored. That was the beginning of what would be two years of disappointment. He said the sloop was still in New Providence but he had arranged passage for us on another sloop that was sailing at high tide that afternoon. I was to dress in men's clothing, James told me, since it was considered unlucky for a woman to be on board.

"It was a difficult eight-day trip from Charles Town to New Providence. We hit rough seas almost as soon as we left Charles Town harbor and I was sick for the first five days of the sailing. All I could keep down was rum and grog and an occasional biscuit I had taken from the plantation. On the first clear day, James and I went on deck. I needed some sun. This gnarly bearded excuse for a man stumbled over to where we were standing and, as he spilled his rum on me, he said, 'This your first shipping? Only a little girl would get sick on these waters!' I looked at James and he started apologizing for me. I pushed James aside and slapped the bully hard on the face and told him that I would see him at sunset right where we were standing and he should bring his sword because he would be fighting for his life.

"I turned and headed for where I had stored my weapons. James was still apologizing for me and took a fist on the chin for not leaving with me. As I unwrapped my swords, James said that I had challenged the second-in-command and he was an expert swordsman. I told James he needed to grow some *nutmegs* and not to worry about me.

"The sun was on the horizon when I arrived where we were to have our confrontation. He showed up carrying a large cutlass. I had my rapier. He cleared some space. Every one of the pirates on the sloop gathered around us.

"He announced that he would make shark meat of this impertinent little girl of a man and laughed loudly. He looked at me and said it was just like a little girl to bring a dagger to a sword fight. Then he snarled. I'm sure he thought this would be easy work. There was a lot of betting going on. I guess I made some of them a lot of money that evening. In the fencing lessons from my father, I had learned to allow the opponent to have the first few moves so that you could evaluate his strengths and weaknesses. I simply dodged his first lunge. That made him laugh. More money was bet. He took a wide swing, which I also dodged. More laughter. He then growled his challenge, 'Are you ready to feel the edge of my cutlass you, little girl coward?' He obviously didn't know I *was* a little girl. To him, he was hurling the ultimate insult.

"It was at that moment that I decided that I would take his ego before I took is life. He started to charge. Again I simply sidestepped his advance and slapped him soundly on the butt with my rapier. He was shocked by the move. The assembled pirates started laughing at him. He made the same move again. And again received a sharp swat on the butt for his effort. Now he was furious. He screamed at me and charged again. Again I sidestepped the thrust but this time I planted my rapier in his side. I quickly withdrew it to be ready for another move but I could hear the air escaping from the wound. I had pierced his lung and I knew he would not stand nor fight again. He jerked a couple of times, crumpled to the deck and was still in death.

"The captain of the sloop walked to the center of the circle and announced that the exhibition was over. He directed two of his crew to strip the corpse of his valuables and clothes and throw the body overboard. He fulfilled his own prophecy. He was the shark meat.

"The captain came to me and suggested I should take the place of the offending pirate as his second-in-command. I declined but said loud enough for all assembled to hear that if anyone gave me any trouble the sharks of the Gulf of Florida would enjoy some more pirate meat.

"James had changed his story as we found our way back to our sleeping space. The same man who was begging for forgiveness for bringing me aboard was now expressing his pride at the way I had fought. I looked him straight in the eyes and said, 'You spineless bastard. You should have been the one fighting.' There was little said between us for the final two days of the trip.

"Sweet Annie, I think it is time to get ready for the evening meal."

Annie asked only one question during the meal. "How old were you, Granny Anne?"

"I was 15. Why?"

"No reason, just curious."

Anne nodded, then motioned for the servants to clean the leavings of the evening meal. As the two women moved toward the porch, she asked for some after-supper coffee to be delivered to where they would be sitting.

They reestablished their positions and allowed a familiar silence to settle in. The coffee arrived and was consumed amidst the quietness.

"Sweet Annie, you said you wanted the real story, are you sure you really want me to continue?"

Pleasantly full from the meal and relaxed from the coffee, Annie's eyes grew bright. "Oh, yes, Granny Anne. More than ever."

"Very well. You remember me saying my next two years were a disappointment. Well, that was an understatement. I learned that practically everything Captain James Bonny had told me was a lie. He wasn't a pirate ship captain. That in itself was disappointment enough. But proving my father right made it especially hard for me. My father was right and I was wrong. Again. When the sloop docked in New Providence, the second of many shoes dropped. We left the sloop and I followed James to our new *home*. It was little more than the brothel room we had shared in Charles Town.

"There I was, newly married, to a liar who wouldn't stand up for me much less himself, and I find that my new home is a small, filthy space in a tent just off Bay Road near where the row boat had dropped us off. I remember saying to James that the slaves at my plantation home lived in better quarters. James said we would look for a better place to live at sunrise. Again, I was disappointed and not very happy with James Bonny. The only positive thing was that I was in the place called the Republic of Pirates so it must be the place where we would find excitement. It was late by then and because of the voyage, all I wanted to do was sleep.

"The next morning, James and I walked around Nassau. There seemed to be a lot of activity, more like what I expected. There were many men walking around dressed like my pirate friends at The Pink House and the 1/2 Moon. James said there were twice as many pirates in Nassau as regular people. It looked that way. My first impression was that Nassau was a filthy town. Charles Town was cleaner. It was August when we arrived. It had rained the day before so the streets and the yards were muddy, in fact everywhere was a muddy mess. Removing garbage didn't seem to be a priority, so there was a rotten smell. And when nature called, that's where it was left. So, the smell of human waste blended with the smell of rotten garbage. No one seemed to mind. It was warm, it wasn't raining. But I was where the pirates were.

"Nassau was an amazing place for pirates to operate from. It was a large, natural harbor. It looked like two hundred, maybe three hundred ships could anchor there. There were many large ships indicating that it was a deep harbor, but there were no ships near the size of a Man o' War and no ships of the Royal Navy nor any Spanish, French, or Dutch war ships—at least none that I saw. There were a lot of fast ships as well—sloops, which were the preferred vessels of the successful pirates.

"I was told some time later that Nassau had become the *Republic of Pirates* for three major reasons—its natural topography, religious politics, and a natural disaster. As I said, it was a large, natural harbor with many natural defenses. There were two entrances. One was very narrow, difficult to navigate, and protected by fort and battery. The other was protected by coral reefs that prohibited the large war ships and many brigantine from entering. Also, only the best navigators, mostly part of pirate crews, could navigate the coral reef protecting the other entrance. Nassau was close to shipping channels and the routes between the Islands and the ports of America, England, Spain, and France.

"Port Royal, Jamaica had been the primary port used by pirates before Nassau. A thriving town had grown up around the port. In 1692, there was a massive earthquake that totally destroyed every building in the town and caused major massive changes in the harbor. The pirate ships that survived had to find a new harbor. Nassau became the harbor of choice.

"Religious politics played a major part in establishing Nassau as the pirates' port. In Europe there was a continuing battle between the English Protestants and the Spanish and French Catholics. In fact, Queen Elizabeth I could be called the creator of the piracy period. She signed *Letters of Marque* establishing privateers, many of whom were members of the Royal Navy. These privateers were actually official pirates of the English Crown whose mission was to capture wealth from Spanish and French merchant ships carrying gold, silver, gems, and later sugar from the islands and deliver it to the English Crown. They operated mainly out of Port Royal on the English (protestant) Island of Jamaica. Spanish Ships were carrying treasures captured from the Aztec, Mayan, Toltec, and Inca people in Mexico and the other mainland areas that bordered the Gulf of Mexico and the Caribbean Sea. The Spanish ships would collect their treasure and outfit in Havana Harbor on the Spanish (Catholic) Island of Cuba for the trip back to Spanish ports. With the disaster in Port Royal, English privateers moved to Nassau since it was close to the shipping channels of the Gulf of Florida. The slow Spanish Galleons were easy targets for the English privateers and the other pirates.

"Nassau grew thanks to this support of the English Crown. Although the English Crown wasn't the origin of piracy, it certainly contributed to its growth in the Caribbean.

"As James and I walked around Nassau, the town did seem alive. It was muddy. It was filthy. It was smelly. But it was alive with people and there was the air of excitement. Nassau had grown along the two roads that made up the town. Bay Road paralleled the Nassau Bay and was where the small boats landed. Bay Road was, like everything else in Nassau, muddy most of the time. It was used by people walking or on horseback most of the time, but there were the occasional horse drawn wagons. Bay Road started at the Battery on Dewitt's Point, went along the waterfront to Spencer's Point on Rushes Bay where it split into two barely passably roads into the inland of New Providence.

"In the center of Nassau, Government Road was a short road that intersected Bay Road and traveled inland a few hundred yards to the Government House built on the top of one of the hills. That was where the Provincial Governor lived and all official business was conducted. There wasn't much of that. There were 45 permanent buildings along Bay Road, 15 or 20 on Government Road and another 30 scattered around the area. Some of these buildings were residences, some were *Groggeries*, and some were brothels and other businesses. The majority of the places where people stayed were little more than tents like the one James found for us. They were everywhere since domestic finery was limited to the wealthy.

"James saw a few people he knew and so did I. I was beginning to feel a little better about being in Nassau.

"A friend of James mentioned that Benjamin Hornigold was gathering a crew for his new sloop, *Happy Return,* and he thought James could find a place on the crew. As it turned out, Hornigold found a place for James. I was left with the wife of one of the crew on the *Happy Return* in a sort of room made of rails tied together with rope. The front was open but had a piece of canvas to give some idea of privacy and keep out some of the rain. The dirt floor was usually mud since it rained almost every day. So, it was filthy and muddy, and like everything else in Nassau, it smelled. The next week the *Happy Return* headed out of the Nassau harbor. I wished James, many Happy Returns. He didn't understand.

"James found a home with Hornigold and for the next six months or so, the *Happy Return* would sail two to three weeks out of every month. They found the waters of the coast of Cuba very productive. Smaller Spanish trading ships were easy targets. They didn't have much in the way of armament and on many occasions they didn't even put up a fight. They usually carried provisions and occasionally money, usually pesos and on rare occasions gold dust. James received his cut of each trip but I soon found that he always brought me only a small part of what he was given.

"I had found a home, if you could call it that, with the other crew members' wives. I was barely able to buy food with the meager money that I was given by James. I met other women who, like me, were married to pirates. In Nassau, men outnumbered women ten to one. These women had the same money problems I had. They tended crops, mended clothes, did laundry, and cooked to make enough money to live on. I had no experience with sewing, laundry, or cooking so I tried working in the fields. I wasn't good at farming, and truth be told, I didn't like the hard work. But if I wanted to find the excitement I was looking for, and that the *groggeries* provided, I needed to make better money.

"The excitement was how I met and married James Bonny and why we were in Nassau, so even though it is something I am now not proud of, I turned to occasional prostitution. I was picky who I went with and actually made pretty good money. Since I had learned that James was keeping some money that he didn't tell me about, I kept the money I made for me.

"Life for James and I had developed into little more than a friendship and not a very good one at that. He minded his own business, and I minded mine.

"Things changed for us in July of 1715. A fleet of 12 Spanish ships sailed from the Havana harbor carrying riches that were difficult to imagine. The registered cargo included 6,388,000 pesos—that was 1,437,000 English pounds sterling. Also, an estimated 955 pounds of gold dust.

"The shipment was supposed to be secret, but everybody in the Bahama Islands, Cuba, Jamaica, and practically everyone else in the entire area knew about the shipment. How do you load that much valuable cargo onto 12 ships and expect it to be secret? That was the *registered* cargo. There were also passengers transporting enormous personal wealth as well. Each of these ships was fully armed, so the shipment alone wasn't of much interest to the pirates of Nassau.

"On July 30th, 1715, however, as the fleet was traveling through the New Bahamas Channel just off the coast of Florida, a hurricane wrecked 11 of the 12 ships. As soon as the news reached Nassau, dozens of pirate ships set out for the area to *fish the wrecks*. The Spanish moved quickly to reclaim as much of the treasure as possible. They established two salvage camps on the coast of Florida close to the sight of the wrecks.

"James had signed on with the Eagle, one of two British ships, sent to salvage as much of the pirate treasure as possible. With the assistance of a captured Spanish navigator who knew where the salvage camps were, the Eagle and a sister ship, the Bersheba, landed between the two salvage camps. The 150 men carried by the two ships were heavily armed. When the pirates arrived at the salvage camps, realizing they were out-numbered and out-gunned, the Spaniards surrendered. The British left the encounter with £27,000 in coinage, 120,000 pesos, seven dozen silver ingots, three bronze swivel guns and 50 copper ingots. James and the rest of the crew were well paid. James brought home enough for us to move into one of the small houses and things were better for a while. I used some of my money to buy a bed and a table and chairs.

"For the next six months, James was gone most of the time, *fishing the wreck*. When the success played out, he came back home.

"It was an inconvenient time for him to return. James caught me in bed with Benjamin West, the Quartermaster of the sloop, *Mary*. He was furious at me and at Benjamin, and he challenged him to a duel. I told James he would have to best me before he could challenge West, and I reminded him of the encounter on the sloop coming to Nassau. Both of my comments made him angry and I'm sure that having me standing naked in front of both my husband and my lover added insult to his injured pride. James told West to get out of his house. West left.

"James told me he had lost respect for me. I told James that he had lost my respect the day I found out the he had lied to me about everything. He told me to shut up, and I slapped him across the face and told him to get his sword because we were going to settle this like men.

"It seemed everything I said made him madder. He grabbed his hat and headed to the door. I told him not to return until he got his head out of his arse or he was ready to fight a duel. It was two days before he finally came crawling back home, begging for forgiveness. Once a spineless bastard, always a spineless bastard, I suppose."

Anne took a long sip of her now cooled coffee and grimaced. She called for a servant to bring a fresh cup. When she looked over at her granddaughter, she saw a faraway look in the younger woman's eyes.

"Well, Sweet Annie, is this boring you?"

"Heavens no, Granny Anne," she paused. "Not at all. I was just thinking that you must have been an absolutely beautiful girl to have men fighting over you. And you were so young. You weren't even as old as I am. I always knew you lived an exciting life but I never imagined…" Annie's words trailed off as the servant returned and handed Anne a steaming cup of black liquid.

"Back to the story. I had little to do with James Bonny for the next year. He had the good common sense to stay out of my way. Had we ever crossed swords he would have been a *Kilkenny cat*. I would have left him naked, with "rat" carved in his chest, missing his manhood, and usable only as a *pegboy*. And he knew it.

"Within weeks of going my own way and leaving James Bonny to his, I met two people who would turn out to be extremely important to me. The first was Pierre Bouspeut. He owned a coffee shop, hairdressing and dressmaking shop, as well as a well-known *MollyHouse*. He was a true artist in velvet and silk material. He taught me a lot about fashion and proper dress. He was a well known *gomorrhean* and took great pride in being called *Pierre the Pansy Pirate*. He became a close friend regardless of his preference for men.

"One thing was certain, he had the ear of some very important people. From one of these people, Pierre learned that a French merchantman ship carrying a huge cargo of costly material would be sailing close by New Providence. I convinced him that we should put a crew together, take a sloop and pirate the ship's cargo. Pierre was hesitant because we couldn't gather any armament, but I developed a plan that I thought would allow us to capture the ship without a battle.

Pierre was absolutely giddy at the thought of capturing a merchant ship with drama instead of weapons.

"Pierre's friends stole a sloop. We meticulously prepared the sloop for our adventure. The crew covered the topsail, deck, and themselves with turtle blood. I took one of Pierre's dressmaker's dummies, dressed it as a woman and covered it with blood. As we went to encounter the ship, I stood in the bow of the sloop over the blood-soaked dummy with a bloody axe. It was a perfect night for the drama. There was a full moon to illuminate our set. So we sailed out to encounter the merchantman. When the crew saw the macabre ship heading for them, they raised a white flag hoping to escape a similar outcome for their ship and crew. We took their cargo without a fight. I still have to laugh when I recall the faces of the crew when we took over their ship. That was the beginning of my love for theater.

"In 1718, Royal Governor Woodes Rogers came to Nassau. The English King had passed a law making piracy illegal. The Governor was sent to enforce that law. At the same time he offered amnesty to any pirate who would turn in his fellow pirates and testify against them, and he would pay them for the information. James Bonny jumped at the opportunity. Remember what I said, *once a spineless bastard...* When he informed me that he was leaving piracy and working as a snitch for the Governor, I threw him out of our house and forbade him to return.

"Then, through my friend Pierre, I met Chidley Bayard. Chidley was one of the richest men in New Providence. He traveled in proper circles. When we met, he was keeping the company of a *hot blooded* Spaniard called Maria Renaldi. I was at my best on that day and Chidley was more than a little interested. Right there in Pierre's coffee shop, Maria challenged me to a duel. I was surprised, but I wouldn't back down. She grabbed a cutlass from one of the pirates there. I saw a pirate with a rapier, my weapon of choice. I casually asked if I could borrow his rapier. Maria was fueled with anger, and that clouded her ability with the cutlass. She took one wild swing which I dodged, and I casually impaled her with the rapier.

"I waited for Pierre and his friends to remove her corpse, then I moved to the seat beside Chidley and asked, 'Is this seat taken?' Always quick witted he answered, 'No, I was saving it for you.' I had found my new home.

"I enjoyed being with Chidley and although I didn't enjoy the people he knew, I enjoyed the parties. With Pierre's help I learned what it was to be a social lady. I remember at the last ball he took me to, he introduced me to the sister-in-law of Jamaican Governor Nicholas Lawes. She was a real bitch. She waited for Chidley to move away to talk to one of his friends, then, she commented that my relationship with Chidley was inappropriate and that I was not worth knowing. She added that I should stay away from her.

"Remember, I had a vicious temper which I had not yet learned to control. I agreed with her and told her I would make sure there was a suitable distance between the two of us. With that, I punched her in the mouth, removing two of her teeth in the process. It caused quite a commotion. I did not regret the punch, but I am sad to say that was the end of my relationship with Chidley.

"I continued to visit my friend's coffee shop, but I spent more time in a local groggerie. Pierre was a good friend and a good source of information thanks to owning the

MollyHouse. One day Pierre asked me to take a walk with him. As we were walking he said he had some information that he thought would be helpful for me to know. One of the visitors to the MollyHouse who'd had too much rum had mentioned a plot to kill Governor Rogers. Pierre said the information couldn't come from him, but that if I were to let Governor Rogers know, it might come in handy for me. In New Providence, you never knew when you might need a friend, and the Governor could be an important friend.

"A few days later I saw Governor Rogers walking not far from his office. I strolled up along side him and mentioned that I had heard of the plot to kill him, and he may need to be extra careful. Sure enough, it wasn't long before three new pirates in Nassau were arrested and hung. Nothing was ever said to me, but I knew I could count on the Governor if I ever needed anything.

"Pierre and Chidley had shown me a little of the sophisticated side of life, and I was starting to enjoy it, but that didn't bridle my temper nor my skills. One night, at the groggerie, I was talking with one of Pierre's friends as I drank my rum. One of the drunken pirates grabbed my arm and suggested that we go crack Jenny's tea cup. He had to be new or he wouldn't have bothered me. He grabbed for my breast—a big mistake. I pushed him away. He tripped over a chair and hit the floor cursing me. Another big mistake. I grabbed the chair he fell over and beat him rather badly with it. One of his friends who knew me pulled him out of the room. I moved back to my drink, 'Now where were we before I was so rudely interrupted?' We went on with our conversation.

"Life without Chidley was boring.

"In the meantime, however, I had met Captain John *Calico*

Jack Rackham, and we found that we had an instant attraction for each other. I didn't know if James had returned or not. I had already moved my clothes and weapons to Jack's house. Meeting *Calico Jack* was the beginning of my life as a true pirate."

The older woman paused in her reverie, allowing the memories which were swirling through her brain to drift into the low country evening fog.

"It is very late, Sweet Annie. This is as good a place as any to stop for the night. I will pick up my life as a pirate tomorrow."

Annie nodded, and together they climbed the stairs to their bedrooms.

Annie's eyes were bright with excitement and a touch of awe as she undressed and brushed out her hair. The inhabitants of the slave quarters were still awake. The strains of their working songs wafted in through the windows, a mournful mix of spirituals and laments for their life of harsh work of the cruelty of the *masser*.

Chapter 7

It was Sunday in Charleston, a day of rest, even for the slaves at Goose Creek Plantation. Chores were few.

Annie was already sitting in the porch swing by the time Anne awoke, and the younger woman had arranged with the cook to have coffee delivered to the table beside her grandmother's rocking chair.

Anne took a moment to savor the rich flavor of the steam cup of coffee, then settled back for what she knew would be a long day of storytelling.

"Where were we?" she asked.

"You had just started the real story of you and Calico Jack, and the true beginning of your life as a pirate," Annie declared. So intrigued was she, that she leaned too far forward in the swing, just as she had a few days before, when she fell on her rump. She almost repeated her performance, before scooting back with an undignified squeak.

The older woman laughed softly, then replied, "So I did. And so I shall pick up with my life with Jack."

"Calico Jack Rackham was everything that James Bonny was not. He was handsome—like James was when we first met. He was English and from a well to do English family. He was educated and experienced in running a ship. He was older than James but not old like the group of pirates in Charles Town. He was a real captain, and he was a real pirate. And he had a *real* house where he lived in Nassau. Not grand like this plantation, but a palace compared to where James expected us to live. The upshot of it all is, Calico Jack was everything I thought James Bonny was, but wasn't.

"They called him *Calico* because he wore nicer clothes than the run of the mill pirates in the region. *His Cool-lots*, what the pirates called the calf-length trousers they wore, were made of colorful calico material, not the common black wool worn by most pirates. I found the calico material was cooler and more comfortable than the black or brown woolen material, especially in the islands of The Bahamas and the town of Nassau. Calico, dyed in many colors, was imported from India, so it was more expensive than the English-made woolen material.

"Young Jack and his family moved from Lincolnshire, England, to Boston in 1696, where his father took the pulpit of one of the unauthorized Baptist churches in the city. Jack's father was a Baptist minister and his mother was a teacher. Jack started law school in 1702. He was well educated by his mother and Boston Latin School, and he was naturally smart. During one of the pox outbreaks in Boston, Jack's mother and father both succumbed to the disease. Jack was left alone to fend for himself. This is the story he relayed to me.

"In 1704, Jack had his law certification, the small house his father had bought in what became the Beacon Hill section of Boston, and no employment. He opened a law practice, but since his father was well known as a Baptist minister, he wasn't able to get many clients because of the prejudice against Baptists—certainly not any of the more moneyed clients.

"In 1705, James Rackham, Esquire, was retained by the Colonial Officials of Boston to represent Captain Thomas

Green, his officers, and crew before the High Court of the Admiralty on the charge of Piracy against the Crown of Great Britain. Regardless of Rackham's excellent defense, the entire group was convicted of Piracy on the High Seas and all were sentenced to hang. On April 4, 1705, pirate Captain Thomas Green was hanged with senior officers James Simpson, Henry Keigle, and George Haines. The penalty for one act of piracy that included 788 grams of gold bars, an unspecified amount of gold dust and 500 grams of silver. The booty was sealed in five leather bags and carried by HMS Guernsey to Great Britain that same year. In losing this legal case, Rackham became aware of the high stakes available to pirates.

"He hung on in his legal practice for four more years. But with mounting costs and little business, he decided he would sell the house, give up the office, and book passage from Boston to New Providence on the fastest sloop in Boston harbor. It took seven days.

"When Jack arrived in Nassau he found a place to stay and prepared to take up the pirate life. His first few days in Nassau he visited many of the *groggeries* and spent the majority of time listening and learning. His Harvard education and law certificate hadn't prepared him for life as a pirate. He had to purchase a cutlass and find someone from whom he could take lessons. He had some natural ability with the cutlass and was soon bettering his instructor. He purchased a pistol and, as he had with the cutlass, became proficient.

"In the meantime, he continued his visits to the *groggeries* and his listened more than he talked, to learn what was happening in the pirate world of Nassau. He soon signed on with Henry Jennings. The year was 1712. Jennings, a British privateer, was based in Jamaica. He had been given his Letters of Marque declaring him an official privateer by the Royal Governor of Jamaica, Lord Archibald Hamilton. Jennings had been educated in England and as such was called *the educated pirate.* Jennings had purchased substantial holdings in Jamaica. No one knew for sure why he had decided to start pirating, but conjecture was that he and his Jamaican wife were having problems. To support that thinking, Lord Hamilton forbade Jennings from returning to Jamaica, although there was substantial evidence that Jennings did return and live in Jamaica some time later.

"During his pirating time on Jennings' ship, the Bersheba, Rackham's education became evident to Jennings, and Rackham was soon named the ship's quartermaster. Rackham and Jennings spent many hours discussing philosophy and law. Rackham's portion of the pirating take was doubled because of the beneficial advice he gave Jennings. Jennings directed the Bersheba to Nassau to give the men a break and the opportunity for some whisky, wenches, and widdles.

"One evening while in port in Nassau, Rackham happened on a meeting between Jennings and Charles Vane, captain of the pirate ship, Ranger. Vane had crewed for Jennings before taking his own ship, which was substantially larger than the Bersheba. Their conversations lasted well into the night. Vane, like Jennings, was born in England and enjoyed an English education. There seemed to be natural chemistry, as well as intellectual chemistry, among the three Englishmen, but it was especially evident between Vane and Rackham. The next year, Vane asked Rackham to join his ship as quartermaster on the *Ranger.* Rackham was paid a triple portion.

"The educational parity benefited Rackham. In addition to his quartermaster duties, Vane would let Rackham captain the ship at times, giving Rackham the practical experience he needed for his next move. That move came sooner rather than later.

"It was November 24, 1718, when Captain Vane refused to challenge a French frigate traveling west of Jamaica reported to be carrying a substantial cargo. It appeared to be armed and Vane didn't want the battle. His decision did not go over well with the crew. They had signed on with Vane for a share of whatever booty their pirating effort yielded. It was called, *no prey—no pay*.

"You might not know, but piracy was an absolute democracy. Majority always ruled. Jack suggested that the only way Vane might be left alive was to allow Jack to call for a vote—sort of like the English Parliament's vote of *no confidence*. Jack assured Vane that if Vane won the vote he would continue to support Vane as captain, but if he lost, Jack would see that Vane would be left alive. Both for his benefit and for peace of the crew, Rackham called for a vote.

"The crew made their decision. Vane was out, and Calico Jack Rackham took over the ship as captain. Jack was true to his word. Vane and a few of his supporters were given a small sloop and enough supplies for a few weeks, and allowed to sail to a nearby island.

"Jack had been considering captaining his own ship for some time and had even designed a distinctive flag for his ship. He told me he wanted it to be a harbinger, an omen, a forewarning of the death that was to come if their challenge was not accepted. His flag was the first to have a large white skull on a black background. The idea was to have a bleached skull to mean death. He added the crossed cutlasses as an afterthought to represent the main weapon of pirates. There was some black and some white material on board the *Ranger*, and Jack used it to make his flag.

"Before they were able to return to Nassau, they encountered a Portuguese galleon. It was taken without a fight. The ship was en route to Havana with its cargo hold filled with casks of fine wine from the island of Madeira off the coast of Africa. Madeira was a valuable cargo. The dark ruby-red wine was aged in special casks and was a secondary cargo on most Portuguese ships, which meant that it stayed in the hold for months which added to the age and quality of the wine. This load had left the port of Funchal ten months before the capture. The extra months of heat and constant rocking of the ship had added to the quality making it a truly fine cargo.

"Madeira was highly valued in the Caribbean and brought a high price from upscale taverns and the elite of the islands. The crew voted on this too. It was decided that each crew member would receive a cask of the fine wine, and the rest would be sold and the income split among the crew. When he returned to Nassau, Jack was flying the flag he called the *Jolly Roger*, and he and the crew were flying high on the spirits of the Island of Madeira and the expectation of a substantial profit from the sale of the rest of the cache.

"So it was that Captain *Calico Jack* Rackham returned to the port of Nassau.

"Now you know the history of Captain John *Calico Jack* Rackham. But I find I'm a bit peckish. Let us go inside for the noon meal, Sweet Annie, and this evening I will pick up with how Jack and I started pirating together."

Chapter 8

True to her word, Anne led Annie back to the porch as the sun began to set, and the women settled into their accustomed placed on the swing and rocking chair. It was obvious that Anne was beginning to enjoy telling and reliving this part of her life.

"My life had become boring without Chidley," Anne declared. "Then I met John Rackham. As I said, Calico Jack was everything that James Bonny wasn't.

"I met Calico Jack in the coffee shop. We met during the time when Jack was living in Nassau covered by the amnesty provided by Governor Woodes Rogers. Pierre introduced us, and Jack took to me instantly. When we were together life was perfect. We became a fixture at Pierre's coffee shop and often visited a number of the local *groggeries* together. Jack had pledged to no longer engage in piracy, but he wasn't too pleased with his life without the excitement that pirating offered. He told me he was going to reclaim the Ranger and was putting together a crew to sail soon.

"That began my insistence on becoming a part of the crew. He finally agreed when I told him that if he left without me, I wouldn't wait for him to return, that our relationship would be over. And he had heard the stories of my ability with sword and pistol, but he had one condition—I had to wear men's clothing and no one could know I was a woman.

"That was nothing new to me, so I became a crew member

and made ready to sail. I must say that I was excited. I was fulfilling my dream of standing beside my man, the captain of a pirate vessel.

"Within the month we set sail. I was known as Bonny and had a somewhat private sleeping place among the other crew members. It was clear to the crew that I was special to Captain Jack by my visits to his cabin. It was normal for a pirate captain to have a special crew member as his pegboy who would visit his quarters on a regular basis. For that reason, most of the crew left me alone.

"However, one day, one of the younger crew members decided that I should service him that evening. I was furious, but realized it was my opportunity to clearly separate me from the rest of the men in that way. I told him that I would meet him at sunset. I showed up with my rapier. With less that a dozen moves his sword was on the deck, his trousers were at his feet and the buttons were missing from his waist-coat. He turned to run and tripped on his trousers. Laying exposed in front of the entire ship, I stood over him with the point of the rapier touching his manhood. I announced if he suggested a gomorrhean adventure with me I would be the *buggerer* and he my pegboy with his manhood missing.

"As he was pulling his trousers up, I turned to the crew and announced, 'Next?' The crew quickly scattered leaving me with Jack. Jack said that I shouldn't have singled out that crew member, but he still thought it was humorous. At least it was something to laugh at.

"Over the next few weeks we encountered a half dozen trading ships, mostly Spanish. We got very little treasure of value, so we took mostly the supplies they were carrying. After a few days with no action, we encountered a brigantine flying a British flag which looked to be around 200 tons. From its slow speed we were certain it was fully loaded. We came alongside her and tossed the grappling hooks and pulled us together. I led the boarding team. The ship had no guns and most of the crew weren't interested in a fight. After we had done away with the first dozen that elected to battle us, the ship was ours. I took out the first two I encountered and the rest of the crew did as well.

"It turns out that ship was carrying gold. A *lot* of gold. The boarding team held the crew at sword point as the rest of our crew moved the gold and other valuable cargo to the Ranger. That was a truly a successful and memorable day.

"I had known Jack for about six months and this was our first pirating adventure together. Not long after our success with the British brigantine, I discovered I was pregnant. There I was, living my life's dream at last, and now being a woman was going to put an end to it. I was devastated. It was the first time I remember crying in front of a man other than my father.

"Jack wanted to take me back to Nassau, but that would end my pirating life. I knew Jack had friends in Cuba, and after much discussion he agreed to take me there until the baby was born, and then we would decide what the future would hold.

"He took me to Cuba. I can't tell you the depth of my disappointment as I watched the Ranger sail out of the harbor with Jack on board and me not.

"Jack's friends were supportive, and I actually warmed to the idea of being a mother. I hoped the baby would be a girl. It was my first experience with these feelings. As my belly grew, I thought less about Jack and more about the baby.

"The birth came early—too early. The babe, a beautiful baby girl, died shortly after she was born. I was certain that I was responsible for her early birth and as a result, her death. I had killed my baby."

Anne's voice cracked and tears welled in her eyes. Annie had never seen this side of her grandmother, and never knew this part of her story. She gracefully rose from the swing and gathered the older woman into an embrace and held her until the tears ceased rolling down her face.

"I'm sorry, Sweet Annie," the older woman managed at last. "I must stop for the night. My heart is too full for words just now."

Annie understood. She nodded without a word, knowing by instinct that words were neither needed nor wanted in this moment. She walked alone up the stairs to her bedroom.

Anne waited a few moments more, allowing the familiar sounds of the plantations to sooth her spirit. At last, she too sought refuge in her bedroom.

It was another sleepless night for Anne. She recalled the regret she had felt at the loss of the little girl, as well as the ache for the loss of her pirating dream. She recalled the countless days, aimlessly walking the sand of Cuban beaches, recurring memories flowing over her consciousness like white-capped Caribbean waves, keeping sleep at bay.

At last the memories of the night gave way to the sounds of the beginning of the day. She gazed out the bedroom window to see the morning fires blazing throughout the slave quarters. Life was returning to Goose Creek Plantation, evidence of the circle of life.

To everything there is a season, she quoted the old book to herself. *And a time to every purpose under heaven. A time to be born and a time to die.*

"The day starts, and the day will end," she said aloud. "This is the start of a new day."

Interlude

PIRACY
A Historical Perspective

This is a little history which the author hopes will help the reader put the acts of piracy in the Caribbean into a historic context, and to understand how and where Anne Bonny fits into that context.

It was 1718 when the world's first female pirate set out on her first *real* pirate adventure. Although pirating in the Caribbean was nothing new—the practice already traced its history back more than two centuries—Anne Bonny was a part of The Golden Age of Piracy.

It is also important to note that piracy was more about the religious, political, economic, and geographic issues than just about the lust for wealth. And there was more to piracy than simply the excitement of the capture and the taking of the wealth that drew young Anne to Nassau. It likely would have come as quite a surprise to young Anne that the center of pirate power wasn't Nassau or even the Caribbean, but Europe. Nor were the most important players any of her buccaneering shipmates, but kings, queens, and Popes.

So, here is the historic thumbnail.

Political

Throughout history, European countries were constantly fighting. Wars between France, England, Italy, Spain, Portugal, Savoy, and Holland were common and required a significant financial commitment. Although the wars were usually over territory, the resulting alliances clouded any clear definitions of the political issues.

Eventually, the European powers started signing treaties that helped bring an end to the Golden Age of Piracy. The treaty of Utrecht was a conglomeration of peace treaties, the first of which was signed April 11, 1713. The process continued until September 7, 1714. As such, the political impetus to clamp down on the pirate trade concluded before Anne made her first pirate voyage.

Religious

Religious issues added to the confusion of the political scene in Europe. The Reformation created religious conflict between England and most of the rest of Europe. October 31, 1517 is considered the culmination of the internal battle in the Catholic Church and the beginning of the Protestant movement in England.

As early as the beginning of 1517, Spain was already taking gold, silver, and gems from the Aztec tribes in what is now Mexico. A substantial portion of the wealth taken from the Aztecs found its way into the coffers of the Catholic Church. Why? Because the Catholic Church had provided *sacred* commissions to the explorers and conquistadors to conquer, annihilate, loot, and, if necessary, kill the native people in the name of The Church in their efforts to convert them, much in the same way they had with the crusaders.

The European exploration and looting in the New World went hand-in-hand with Catholic missionary endeavors to convert it. Some of the most trusted and best educated priests were sent to the New World. It should be noted that many Catholic priests objected to and spoke out against the harsh treatment of the indigenous people at the hands of the conquistadors.

The Protestant Reformation swept over Europe in the early 1500s, along with King Henry VIII's break with the Pope and the Catholic Church over the annulment of his marriage to Catherine of Aragon so that he could marry Anne Boleyn. This break ultimately resulted in the establishment of the Church of England.

England was at war with the Catholic Church and most of the countries in Europe. Remember, war is expensive.

ECONOMIC

An additional influence on the success of piracy in the Caribbean was slave trade. Cotton, rice, and indigo plantations in America needed workers. So did the sugar plantations in the Caribbean. In order to grow their influence, European powers captured lands in Africa, and in the process enslaved the indigenous people and sold them to plantation owners.

Each slave was a valuable commodity. When a pirate captured a ship that was transporting slaves, they herded the slaves into the pirate ship along with the gold, silver, gems, and provisions. Pirates made deals with the slave sellers and earned a commission on each slave they delivered.

The political, economic, religious, and financial issues in Europe contributes greatly to the environment in which our main character found herself.

Geographic

All of the major pirate ports were in close proximity to the Gulf Stream—what pirate ship captains called *the river within the sea*. The main ports of the 1500's were Havana, Cuba, and Port Royal, Jamaica. The port at Port Royal (near what is now Kingston) was totally destroyed in the earthquake of June 7, 1692.

The Spaniards operated out of the large, deep harbor of Havana, Cuba. The conquistadors and explorers were able to utilize small ships to access and loot Aztec towns and villages along the coast of the Yucatan and northward.

English buccaneers initially operated out of Hispaniola but needed a port nearer the Spanish shipping avenues. Port Royal, Jamaica, became the center of English piracy in the Caribbean, until the earthquake of 1692 destroyed the port. Pirates in general moved their activities to Nassau Harbor on the island of New Providence, which was ideally situated between Cuba and European ports and on the narrow Straits of Florida used by all ships headed to Europe.

The only difference between a pirate and a privateer was an official document called a *Letter of Marque* issued by any government.

Timing

Timing was also a primary contributor to Anne Bonny's

success as a pirate. Anne Bonny arrived in Nassau in 1716. She was a 17-year-old girl when she joined the *Brethren of the Coast* in 1718. But piracy had already reached its peak in 1715 according to many authorities, and was actually on its way out by the time Anne arrived and signed the *Articles of Agreement*—often referred to in popular culture as *The Pirate Code*. Prior to her first sail as a pirate, King George 1 (King of England 1714–1727) had outlawed piracy. Two of the most infamous pirates had already been captured. Edward Teach, commonly known as Blackbeard, was captured November 22, 1718, and his head was cut off and hung on the bowsprit of Lieutenant Robert Maynard's sloop *Ranger*. Stede Bonnet, The Gentleman Pirate, was captured by Colonel William Rhett September 26, 1718, and hanged at low water's mark on White Point Gardens in Charles Town.

The only way for the European governments to regain control of the sea was through strong, harsh dealings with pirates and piracy. In the decade between 1716 and 1726 as many as 600 pirates were captured and executed. *Calico Jack* Rackham was among them. Without the aid of some influential friends, Anne Bonny would have been hanged as well.

Now, back to our story.

Chapter 9

Anne had little to say the next morning. Her mind was on the little girl she buried in Cuba. She and Annie performed their routine chores. Life on the plantation hummed along as it had before Anne revealed the devastating details of that previous chapter of her story. She skipped the noon meal, but agreed to meet with Annie to review the plantation books, as was their custom. By the time she sat down to the evening meal Anne had recovered much of her normal humor, and seemed more like her old self.

Still, conversation during the meal was subdued. As they left the table, Anne took Annie by the hand and apologized for her demeanor. "I am sorry, Sweet Annie. It has been many years since I have thought of that time in Cuba. I suppose I still had some more crying to do."

They returned to the porch swing and rocking chair, and Anne resumed her tale.

"I buried the baby—my baby girl. I spent many a day walking the beach, weeping. There were days of crying. There were days of silence while I waited for Jack to return. There were days when I felt nothing at all. Eventually, I cried myself out—or so I thought.

"Finally I saw the *Ranger* at a distance. A small landing boat was lowered and a single figure rowed to the beach. Jack had returned.

"Then there were more tears. I told Jack the story of losing the baby and we discussed what we would do now. We decided that losing the baby would allow us to continue our plans and our dreams. That was a sad day but also a happy one.

"It was on the way back to Nassau that I decided I had hid the fact that I was a woman long enough. I discussed it with Jack. He agreed but suggested that it would be best for me and the current crew if I waited until the next sailing to reveal my womanhood. Reluctantly I agreed. I could stay a man for a few more days.

"On the way back to Nassau we encountered a sloop similar to the *Ranger,* but it was sitting very low in the water. We knew it had to be loaded. We came along side, tossed the grappling hooks, and I prepared to board it as I had many times before. It was the initial encounter that showed me that my stay in Cuba had taken its toll on my skills with my rapier. A young sailor I encountered gave fight. One of his blows knocked the rapier from my hand. He had his cutlass at my throat, and I knew I was done for."

"Granny Anne, what did you do?" Annie couldn't suppress her outburst.

The older woman chuckled at the memory. "I had an inspiration. I ripped open my waistcoat to expose my breasts. The sight of them caused the young fellow to lose his concentration for a moment. That was all the opportunity I needed to draw my pistol and fire. I thought I saw a smile cross his face as he collapsed. Perhaps it was the image of my breasts that was his last thought as he fell dead on the deck.

"We captured that ship and removed a valuable cargo of gold and silver—but there was no keeping my secret now. I stayed in Jack's quarters for the rest of the voyage. We unloaded the treasure on Hog Island. We divided the shares and re-boarded the *Ranger*, and to the best of my knowledge nothing was said about a woman being on board the sloop.

"I returned to Jack's house. I knew I needed some time to train with my rapier again. My skills may have suffered from my time in Cuba, but my attitude and temper were still razor sharp. As I regained my skill, and my confidence and wit returned as well. I started calling Jack, *My Jack*, especially when he was being stubborn, which was most of the time. There were many Jacks in New Providence but most were tied to posts in barn yards. He knew exactly what I meant, but he also knew it was in jest.

"Things were going along quite pleasantly. Jack needed to take care of some business dealing with the sloop, and I decided I wanted to visit my friend Pierre. I suppose James saw me. Once a spineless bastard, always a spineless bastard, Bonny had recruited four of his friends to abduct me. It took all five of them to overpower me, but I left some marks and sore places on each of them. They took me before the Governor where James charged me with felony desertion. I was thrown into jail.

"The Governor couldn't ignore my infidelity, nor could he let me go unpunished. James had developed a friendship with the Governor, and he wanted me hanged. He wanted Jack hanged as well.

"Jack came to the Governor's office with a proposal—he offered to buy my freedom, or at the very least he suggested have a bidding competition between himself and James. That wouldn't have been much of a contest. James never had any money.

"At James' insistence I was stripped naked and compelled to stand there before the honorable Governor Woodes Rogers, in addition to James, Jack, and a dozen or so other people. It appeared that James wanted to embarrass me. Apparently, he had forgotten that I was absolutely comfortable standing naked in front of him and Benjamin West. Most of the people in the room had already seen me naked, so why he thought I would be embarrassed was beyond my understanding.

"Women were considered chattel, or property. In the eyes of the law I was considered stolen property, and the governor was compelled to uphold the law. But James Bonny wasn't the only one who had cultivated a friendship with Governor Rogers. As you may recall, I had once provided him with valuable information concerning the plot to kill him. You might say I had saved his life, and he hadn't forgotten it. He decided to be lenient. My only punishment was that Governor Rogers forbade me from seeing Jack. I am certain he knew before he said it that was a waste of his breath.

"James was furious—and more than a little afraid. He screamed at the governor, 'She'll kill me if she is set free!'

"To his credit Governor Rogers calmly answered him, 'Then she'll hang for your murder.' Then, in a surprise move, the governor rose from the judgment seat, walked up to James, and said face-to-face, 'Are you so afraid of her?' Everyone in the office knew the answer.

"James cursed me, then he cursed Jack and walked out of the Governor's office. As he walked past me he whispered, 'Just give me half a chance and I will kill you and hang your naked body upside down on a tree in front of *Calico Jack* Rackham's house for all to see, you low class *strumpet*.'

"I let him get a few feet from me and said loud enough for everyone in the room to hear, 'So you are challenging me?

Get your sword and let's settle this like men, you spineless bastard. It took you and your four *barmy* friends to get me here. Look at that one, his face is so messed up he may never be the same.' James left the room without answering.

"I told Jack that I was going to Pierre's to get something to wear and I would see him at home.

"We both knew that we couldn't stay in Nassau. We had pushed the Governor about as far as we could. We finalized our plans to acquire and outfit the *Kingston*, gather a crew, and get out of New Providence. Before nightfall, Jack had gathered nine of his former crew members. He arranged for them to meet us at sunrise. The *Kingston* had been brought near Nassau at a place where it wasn't obvious with a week's provisions loaded on board. Jack had already told the crew that I would be on board as a woman and since each had seen me in action, there wasn't a problem. Since I had experience keeping the plantation books, it was natural for me to be assigned the role of the Quartermaster. And so it was, that as I had dreamed, I was standing next to my man, the captain of a real pirate ship.

"The next morning we sailed past the town of Nassau and out of Nassau Town Harbor, through the Great Channel of Providence and into the Gulf of Florida headed for Cuba. I insisted that we fly Jack's flag as we left the Nassau harbor. It was my statement to the spineless bastard, James Bonny. I was standing next to Captain *Calico Jack* Rackham and I had stripped to my waist, proudly displaying the symbol of my womanhood.

"We knew that we needed to capture the first ship we saw to fully stock our ship's store for more than a week. Luck was on our side. We encountered a small brigantine flying the Spanish flag. It wasn't armed so we pulled along side, tossed the grappling hooks, and we boarded her. Only two of its crew made an attempt to defend the ship. They paid for that effort with their lives. We emptied the provisions, leaving enough for a few days to get them to a nearby port. We hadn't expected to take any treasure, but there was a stock of gold doubloons. I estimated there to be about 1,000. The hand-minted coins looked to be Mexican, so each doubloon would have contained seven grams of gold. 7,000 grams of gold and a fully stocked ship's store was a very good first day pirating. Each crew member got a double ration of rum, so they were happy.

"We pirated a number of small cargo ships and a few fishing boats. They were not armed and gave our boarding team little resistance. The majority of the cargo ships had small crews, and they weren't paid very much so they weren't willing to bet their lives that they were better swordsmen than the pirates. It was like picking cherries.

Anne glanced at her granddaughter, and marked the glistening admiration in the girl's eyes. She have her a quick smile and a nod.

"Sweet Annie, look at that ring around the moon. We will be having some rain tomorrow. Let's retire. We'll pick back up tomorrow, and I will tell you about the closest call Jack and I had before we were captured."

Again the pair climbed the stairs holding hands. They hugged at the top of the stairs and went to their respective rooms. Anne paused as she was lowering the window of her bedroom. *The plantation needs some rain*, she thought. There was a light flash to the south of the plantation. *Over the ocean*, she thought.

She started counting the seconds—*eight, nine, ten, eleven, twelve* —just as she pronounced *thirteen*, there was a loud clap of thunder. Mentally she divided the seconds by five and said aloud, "The storm is just a little over two and a half miles away to the south, over the ocean."

Knowing how far a storm was away was helpful in getting the plantation ready for rain. She walked back downstairs and told the kitchen helper to send word to William that a thunderstorm was about an hour away and to make sure the horses were prepared.

Back in her bedroom, she again looked out of the window to see a number of lanterns scurrying around the barn. Soon all of those lights were doused, and she turned toward the bed.

Another flash—*four, five, six, seven, eight.* This time the thunder clap rattled the windows. She knew the storm was a mile and a half away and would be at the plantation in about 20 minutes. The weather was something her father always watched, and this valuable little piece of information was something he had taught her. It had come in handy on the plantation as well as during her short pirating career.

Anne slipped out of her clothes and prepared her bed for the night. As she slipped between the cotton sheets, she heard the first sounds of rain pelleting against her bedroom window. She drifted into sleep thinking, *Tomorrow will be a good conversation with Sweet Annie.*

Chapter 10

It was a subdued, gray morning light that greeted Anne Cormac to the world of Goose Creek Plantation. The driven rain that began the previous evening had settled into an easy steady rainfall—*a soaking rain,* the farm slaves called it.

Annie was still asleep when Anne walked down the grand staircase on the way to the kitchen. The rain hitting the tin-covered walkway from the main house to the kitchen house resonated with a soft tattoo announcing a day that would be more rest than work.

It was at least an hour later before Annie descended the stairs still attired in her night clothes, and joined her at the dining table for morning coffee and breakfast. Anne started to send her back upstairs to get properly dressed, but decided that since only the house slaves and possibly William would be in the house she would let this breach of etiquette go unchallenged.

"Sweet Annie, since the rain has limited our chores this morning, let's do the plantation books first thing this morning after breakfast and start story time after our noon meal."

Annie nodded. Breakfast turned into quiet time for Anne and Annie, each wrapped in their own thoughts, as the rain drummed its drowse-inducing rhythm. Annie finally slid off her chair and sauntered upstairs to dress, while Anne moved to the office to discuss operations with William and the plantation foreman.

By the time Annie returned, Anne had dismissed the servants and was already working on the books. Soon the smell of hearty vegetable soup interrupted the business of the plantation. Neither Anne nor Annie could have told where the time had gone, but it was near noon, so Anne called an end of their business meeting and rang the bell ordering the noon meal to be served.

Luncheon developed into a playful session between the two women. Memories of fun times were punctuated by questions Annie had about the ongoing story of Anne's adventurous life. Anne deferred answering until they finished eating and moved back to their accustomed places on the porch. A chill in the air prompted Anne to send for the lamb's wool coverlets. Comfortably full and warm against the damp air, Anne resumed her tale.

"It was my first trip as the ship's quartermaster. I remember it well. I was the second-in-command—sort of like the assistant captain. Jack was a very good captain. He was seasoned as a navigator. He knew where we needed to go and how to get there. Jack had decided that this sailing would be to Cuba. Cuba was like his second home. He knew the waters like the back of his hand. We had a filled ship's store, a good crew, and a stock of munitions. Everybody was ready for some excitement, me included.

"So, we set sail. The area around Trinidad was always good pirating waters, and Jack knew well the waters on the southern side of Cuba. Trinidad was quite a distance from the main harbor of Havana, therefore not likely to have military presence. The closest port was Cienfuegos, but there were many small deep water bays and inlets in that part of the island near Trinidad. In the early years of piracy, Trinidad was a favored port for Spanish conquistadors as they gathered treasure from the Aztec people.

"We decided to focus our efforts there for a number of reasons. It was the center of sugar production. Valle de los Ingenios, or the valley of the sugar mills, was just outside the port, and where there is sugar production, there is rum production. Slave ships were constantly headed for Trinidad to provide labor for the sugar plantations, merchant ships were constantly leaving the port filled with sugar and rum, and there was a thriving commercial area selling goods to fill ship's stores.

"Jack had decided to keep one of the faster fishing boats we had captured because it was an especially nice small sloop. We had it in tow, sort of as a back-up.

"On our way to Trinidad we met a Spanish merchant galleon headed for Cadiz, Spain. Our store was fully stocked but we did take a lot of their rum. Since the crew caused us no problems, Jack took the rum and let them continue on their way. That turned out to be a reckless move. For the next couple of days the crew, Jack, and I drank the rum and relaxed. Then the tables turned. The captain of the galleon had changed his course and sailed to Cienfuegos where he alerted the Spanish officials there.

"A Spanish coastal guard ship was dispatched to the area where we had overtaken the galleon. It was almost sunset when the guard ship arrived. Our crew were mostly hung over from an over-indulgence in pirated rum. The appearance of the guard ship was a big surprise, but it was too late in the evening to begin a battle. Jack had anchored the *Kingston* and the small sloop in a protected bay behind a small island. The Spanish guard ship had laid anchor in the center of the narrow channel entrance to the bay where we were. The guard ship appeared to be fully armed and we would have been no match for it in a battle. I'm sure the Spanish captain knew this so he simply blocked our exit and waited for first light.

"I thought we were done for. There was no apparent means of escape. We would have been in big trouble if it had not been for the ingenuity of *My Jack*. He came up with a marvelous plan.

"We moved the treasure and one week's food to the fishing sloop. The sloop was fitted with oars so we wrapped the oars with sail cloth and silently rowed the sloop past the guard ship. Thankfully, there was a new moon, and clouds covered the stars. We waited until midnight, then rowed silently away. At one point we were no more than the width of one ship from the guard ship. No one even noticed us. It was a bold move on our part. I don't think I have ever been more proud of *My Jack*.

"By first light, we were miles away from the bay and the fierce Spanish guard ship, the proud *Guardia del Costa*. I only wished that I could have been there when the Spanish boarding party climbed on board the *Kingston*, weapons at the ready, only to find a totally deserted ship. We laughed all of the way back to Hog Island where we divided the loot.

"Jack sent one of the small boats we kept at Hog Island with the crew on board into Nassau. We gave them a week to enjoy some whiskey, wenches, and widdles. Jack and I decided to stay on the sloop to have some time together. Since the fishing boat didn't have an acceptable pirate name, Jack insisted on calling the sloop, *Miculo*. 'Let's eat on *Miculo*,' he would say. That was the source of some humor over the next couple of weeks.

"After a week in Nassau the crew were ready to get back to buccaneering. Truth be known, so were Jack and I. We had enough food and rum to last a few weeks, so we set sail for the main shipping route, the channel between New Providence and the Florida mainland.

"Unbeknownst to me, I was heading into the next chapter of my life as a pirate and as a woman.

"We encountered our first prey the day after leaving our protected Hog Island harbor. It was a mid-size merchant ship, a Dutch *fluyt*, on it's way to Cienfuegos from the Gold Coast of Africa with a full load of slaves bound to the sugar plantations on the southern coast of Cuba. Jack thought it would be an easy mark because it would be manned by a small crew. He was wrong.

"The Dutch had a unique design for their *fluyts*—a design that allowed the ships to carry more cargo and required half the crew of similar size ships manufactured by the English and Spain. The Dutch ship's captain was skilled in evading our efforts to come along side and throw our grappling hooks. But, *My Jack* was a suitable match and we were able to board and subdue the Dutch crew. That is when our initial problem started—the crew spoke only Dutch. None of our crew spoke Dutch and none of their crew spoke any of the languages our group spoke. Then we caught a break. One of their crew, a fellow named Mark, admitted that he spoke both Dutch and English, when it became obvious that we would have killed the entire crew if we couldn't communicate.

"I had noticed him when I boarded the ship. Even though he was a strong and intense fighter, he had a certain charm about him. Jack and I surveyed the ship. We both knew that *Miculo* couldn't meet our needs for very much longer, so we were looking to see if we could take over the Dutch ship and convert it for our needs. We discussed taking the ship to Charles Town where we could get a handsome price for the slaves. That settled it. We decided to put the Dutch crew on the smaller boat, and set sail for Charles Town on our new ship. I reminded Jack that it wouldn't be a good idea for me to be seen in Charles Town, but he could meet with our contacts to sell the slaves.

"I asked Jack what he was going to do with Mark, the fellow who had helped with the translation. Jack said if he would sign the Articles of Agreement he could join our crew. After Mark agreed to sign, Jack told Mark to make the same offer to the slave master. He agreed. Mark was put in charge of the slaves, but the slave master answered to Mark.

"Sweet Annie, here I must confess that for the rest of the cruise to Charles Town, I couldn't get Mark out of my mind. Making love with Jack that evening was a physical release, but I was thinking about Mark the entire time. I knew I had to be careful, but I was absolutely fascinated by this new sign-on.

"Not that Mark encouraged my attention. He mostly kept to himself. He was almost standoffish, and that made him even more interesting to me. I started looking for reasons to be where he was. I was as fascinated by Mark as I had been when I first met James.

"We took the captured slaves to the agreed upon transfer point near Charles Town. Jack, Mark, and most of the crew moved the slaves to the slave brokers ship. I stayed out of sight and we were able to conclude our business and leave Charles Town harbor without being recognized as a pirate vessel, mostly because our new ship was flying the Dutch flag. So it was, we set sail for Cuba with a substantial bounty from the sale of the pirated slaves.

"Two small traders were taken on our way to Cuba. One had unloaded all of its cargo in Charles Town, so all we got was some supplies, a stock of gunpowder, and some rum. But the other was on its way to Charles Town. We put its cargo of sugar where the slaves had been.

"We had been under sail for about a week when it finally happened. Mark and I were on night watch. No one else was up and about. As you may remember me telling you, I was a real flirt. I would ask Mark questions to coax him into conversation, even though he wasn't very talkative. I eventually got him to relax, and once he even laughed out loud. My dear Sweet Annie, you would have been proud of the girl I became for a short time that night.

"The time was right. There was a lull in the conversation. There was a full moon. Each of the ripples on the sea surface caught the reflection of the moonlight and made the backdrop look like a sea of fireflies. The night was perfect. The time was perfect. I reached over and kissed Mark. It caught him by surprise. He drew back for a moment, but then tenderly kissed me back. It was like the first time I kissed James—magical.

"Remember, I was openly a woman at that time. And Mark, to me, was all man. A few awkward moments passed as we parted and considered each other. I was the ship's quartermaster, second-in-command—and he knew that I was the captain's woman. But he also knew we had shared a special moment. I suppose it took a great deal of courage for him to reveal that *he* was a *she*. That's right, Sweet Annie. *Mark* was actually *Mary*.

"I was taken aback as well, I can tell you that. I had just

sought after and kissed another woman. At that moment it was awkward for both of us, yet we couldn't deny that there was a connection that had occurred. Praise be to all that is holy that at just that moment the late night watch showed up to relieve us.

"I was confused, to say the least. I went to the cabin I shared with Jack, and Mary walked to the sleeping area she shared with the rest of the crew, each of us fully captured in our own thoughts.

"Jack was sound asleep when I entered the cabin. I welcomed the opportunity to being alone with my thoughts. I hoped that sleep would walk into the cabin with me, but sleep wasn't interested in delivering me from my dilemma. I was awake all night long.

"I couldn't understand why I was so interested in a woman when I was with the man I thought was the man of my life. What could I do? What *would* I do? Just two of the many questions that were dueling inside my brain. Still, I couldn't deny what had just happened. There *was* a chemistry between us. I was awake until the wee hours of the morning.

"Mary later confided to me that she had experienced much the same as I did.

"I avoided being alone with Mary after that. As you can imagine, that was a chore, considering how small a ship is. There weren't a lot of places to hide, and hiding was exactly what I was doing. I was hiding from Mary, and I was hiding from my own feelings.

"At last I asked Mary to meet me in the bow of the ship. It was the one place where we could have a little privacy. It was awkward at first. I told her that this was the first time for me, having feelings for another woman.

"I said, 'You know, what we are talking about is illegal.'

"There was a pause, then Mary looked at me and said, 'What we do every day is illegal.'

"That little bit of humor sort of broke the ice and we both laughed. There we were, two pirates, talking about a personal relationship being illegal when we regularly killed people and stole from them. Oh, well. We continued the conversation.

"I decided that it was important for us to see if there was more between us. Mary agreed. She said, 'We have to have some time together, alone.' I agreed.

"As if fate was listening to us that opportunity presented itself two days later. Jack said we had to put into port to restock the ship stores. He said he would make the town trip because he could get better deals on supplies than I could. Normally I would have argued with him since the ships stores were my responsibility, but I realized that fate had provided the opportunity to be with Mary, uninterrupted.

"Jack left the ship along with most of the crew. Mary and I were left with two new sign-ons. I assigned them first watch and hurried to meet Mary in the cabin I shared with Jack.

"I think we were both excited and anxious. I know I was. We were out of our clothes and into the bunk in seconds—at least that is the way I remember it. I had heard stories of women coupling with women, that it was better because a woman knows how to pleasure another woman. I can tell you for a fact, that was not true for us. We both tried to pleasure and gain pleasure for at least an hour before we decided that we were not going to be successful as lovers. We were tentative to begin with, neither taking charge. Then we both tried to take charge. Nothing seemed to work. I was on the verge of tears, which was not a common experience for me.

"I was more than disappointed. I had expected so much. I just wanted to hit something or someone. Neither of us wanted to talk about it. We dressed and walked to different parts of the ship to sulk privately.

"Before the others returned we did talk about it, and came to the conclusion that while there was a connection between us, it was not one that could be gratified by sexual adventures. I respected Mary's swordsmanship, or should I say swords-*woman*ship, and her abilities as a pirate, and I told her so. She said she thought of me in the same way and she would protect me at any battle. The upshot is that we decided that we could be shipmates and friends, but not lovers.

"I asked her if I could confide the fact that she was a woman to Jack. She knew that Jack was open to treating a woman pirate equally to a man pirate since he had with me, so we agreed. We went out to the deck to join the other crewmembers who were on watch. Within a few hours Jack returned and we prepared to set sail.

"Well, Sweet Annie, I think this is as good a place as any to stop for the day. Tomorrow I will tell you about the most dangerous of our adventures—the taking of the William. But for now I'm talked out. Let's go to bed.

Annie sat breathless and bright-eyed.

"Granny Anne, it's hard for me to believe you had a relationship with another woman."

"Mary became my very close friend. We would be in prison together. But I wouldn't say we had a *relationship*, at least not in that way. At that time I was quite young, only two years older than you are now. If we had both been older, or if our situation had been different, who knows. What I did learn is to never say never. But I'm getting hoarse, I need to stop talking."

Anne and Annie, again, walked hand in hand up the stairs to the second floor of the plantation house. Again, they split at the landing, heading to their bedrooms in silence. Anne stopped before entering her room. She turned facing the direction of Annie's room where her granddaughter had already entered her room and closed the door. Anne said aloud but just above a whisper, "I love you, Sweet Annie. I hope telling you the story of my life hasn't been a bad idea. I love you more than life itself. I wouldn't want this story to change our relationship."

With that, Anne Cormac opened her own bedroom door and entered the room. It was like she had stepped into a different dimension. Her routine was the same, but all of the actions had slowed. She was light headed. She undressed and slipped between the sheets as the room started slowly revolving. She closed her eyes, hoping that would stop the spinning. She opened them but the carousel that was her room continued in that slow 360-degree circuit around her bed. There was a dull ache in her head and her throat felt like a small circus performer was scrubbing it with sandpaper. Anne reached into the chest beside her bed and extracted a bottle of medicinal *Kill Devil*, the name given to strong rum. Kill Devil was known to cure a variety of diseases but especially the disease you got from breathing *bad air*. There were many people who believed that Charles Town was filled with opportunities to breathe bad air.

After the fifth swallow of Kill Devil, Anne was certain she had consumed enough of the liquid provided to her by her family doctor in Charles Town to cure the problems of breathing bad air and pretty much anything else that ailed her. She set the cork back in the glass bottle and put it back on her bedside cabinet. She took a deep breath and everything seemed better. She lay back down and soon all of the devils were on the deceased list.

Chapter 11

Morning arrived after a much too short night. The symptoms of breathing bad air had been replaced by the symptoms of drinking too much Kill Devil. Anne's head still hurt. Now her eyes hurt. Her ears hurt. Her stomach hurt. Her teeth hurt. But her throat was as good as new.

Annie knocked on her bedroom door to inquire if she were all right. It was well after her normal awakening time. Annie smiled. She knew the results of overindulging in the medicinal rum. With the Kill Devil bottle sitting in full view on the side cabinet, Anne's problem was obvious. Annie leaned over the bed and hugged her grandmother and suggested she close her eyes and go back to sleep.

Sleep she did.

It was mid-afternoon when Anne again opened her eyes. Her mouth was dry, and she needed the chamber pot, but those were the only lingering problems from her battle with the devil. As she listened to the soft splashing evidence that she was using the chamber pot, she thought of an old saying, "If you play with the devil you have to pay the devil." She finished and covered the pot.

She poured water in the washbasin, dampened a nearby cloth, and wiped her face with the cool, soothing liquid. She again dipped the cloth in the water basin and bathed her face. One more time. Then the back of her neck.

"Ah," she heard herself say aloud. She knew it was time to

start her day, even though it was mid-afternoon. Anne walked downstairs and encountered Annie and William sitting at the dining room table working on the budget for the horses.

Annie was the first to speak. "How are you feeling, Granny Anne? You look like you are feeling much better."

"I had a rough night, Sweet Annie. By the time I got to my room last night, I knew I was sick. Breathing bad air, I reckon. But I had a bottle of Kill Devil and I suppose it worked. I took three doses and I slept like a baby. This ache in my head suggests that I should have stopped at two. Right now what I want is a cup of coffee and a little *fresh* air."

Annie accompanied Anne, holding her cup of coffee in shaky hands, to the front veranda. Annie jumped into the swing. Anne slipped gingerly into the rocker. Anne took a deep breath. Then another. And one more before she began talking to her granddaughter.

"Sweet Annie, I am concerned that the story of my life is giving you a bad picture of your grandmother. I have done some questionable things in my life, but because I agreed to tell you the true story that is what I am doing. I fear I am perhaps telling you more than you want to hear."

Anne paused, took a sip of the hot coffee, and looked into her granddaughter's eyes. Annie returned her gaze, but offered no objection. Anne nodded, then picked up her story from where she had left off the night before.

"You already knew that I had killed a few men in my day—maybe more than a few." Anne paused again and sipped the coffee as if formulating what to say next—or how to say it. "I want you to realize that my life as a pirate, and my experience with Mary, and—well there a few other things—they all happened when I was very young, and I had no rules that I lived by. I don't regret any of my actions, especially my experience with Mary. In fact, she became my closest friend. I don't regret any part of my life, although truth be told, if I could live my life over there are some things that I would do differently. I learned from every experience. And, I am the woman I am today because of the girl I was then." Anne took another deep breath, another sip of coffee, and sat for a moment in silence.

"No, no, no, Granny Anne." Annie was again sitting very close to the edge of the swing. She caught herself before she fell. "You are a marvelous woman and I really want to know everything you are willing to tell me. Everything."

"I know you and William reviewed the plantation books this morning, but I need to check on the colt and get a little something to eat. We shall return to the story this evening, if that is alright with you?" Anne looked over at the barn.

"Whatever you say, Granny Anne."

Although Anne was feeling better, she walked upstairs and retrieved her trusty bottle of Kill Devil for one small drink before she ventured out to the barn.

The colt was jumping around, full of life. That was something Anne liked to see at the plantation. It was like a reaffirmation of life itself. It was, to her, proof that the circle of life was alive and well at Goose Creek Plantation. Having Annie at the plantation carried the same purpose—the assurance that another generation will carry on the tradition.

Anne watched the colt for a few more moments. Annie walked up and stood next to her grandmother. She, too, watched the colt frolic. The two women shared the moment in silence. Anne reached out and embraced her granddaughter.

"I love you, Sweet Annie."

"And I love you Granny Anne, but I came here to tell you that the evening meal is ready."

Anne and Annie walked hand in hand back to the plantation house. Anne went upstairs to dress for dinner, as was her custom. Annie was already seated at the table when Anne arrived. The meal was served and the pair ate with no conversation. Annie was the first to break the silence.

"Did you know Mary Reid very long? I don't remember hearing you talk about her before."

"Not really, but we went through so much together that it seemed like we had been friends for a large part of my life." Anne paused. "It couldn't have been more than six months that we worked together on Jack's ships, and another six months in prison together. But the time in prison seemed like an eternity."

"Will you tell me more about her?"

There was another pause.

"Finish your meal and we will go back out to the veranda."

"Well, Sweet Annie, this is the story of Mary Reid, as I remember it from what she told me. Some of our conversations occurred when we were adventuring together on board ship when nothing was happening, but she told me most of her story while we sat on the floor of that filthy Jamaican prison.

"Just like me, Mary's parents weren't married. That didn't seem to matter much to either of us. She was born in Plymouth, England, in 1685. Mary was the second child. She had an older brother, her mother's legitimate child. His father was married to Mary's mother but he left her while she was pregnant. The young boy died when he was six. Mary was five at the time. Hoping to get some money from her former husband's mother, Mary's mother dressed her as a boy and tried to convince her mother-in-law that Mary was her *grandson*. The amazing thing was that she was successful. The grandmother gave Mary's mother a crown each week to feed and take care of her *grandson*. It appears that Mary was good at being a boy.

"Mary's mother died when Mary, as Mark Reid, was still a teenager. There was no work for a teenage girl in England at that time, so Mary, continuing her disguise as a boy, was hired by a French woman to be her *footman*. Still, no one was the wiser. When she was no longer needed as a footman, Mary/Mark got a job as a *cabin boy* in the French Navy. Mary was good enough impersonating a young man that she was able to switch to the Flemish Army. She spoke English and French, and quickly picked up Dutch.

"Mary was a fierce fighter, a good shot, and extremely well qualified with a sword. Unable to get a commission in the army, she joined the cavalry. Turned out she was as good a horsewoman as she was as a fighter.

"Finally her hormones won out. She fell in love with her tentmate, also a cavalryman. She finally confided to him that she was a woman and that she loved him. It was then she found out that he had been attracted to her, but didn't know how to deal with those emotions with another man. They decided to get married.

"Their commander couldn't have a female member of his troop, so he agreed for them to leave the regiment to get married. Following the marriage, the pair opened a public house, Three Trade Horses, in the town of Breda, Holland, not far from Rotterdam. It soon became the favored eating-place of many Flemish officers, who ate with them regularly. They were very successful for a while. Mary said she was happy in her role as a wife. But two things happened that caused Mary to again take on the clothes and identity of a man.

"First, Mary's husband died unexpectedly. Second was the Dutch military signed a peace treaty, which caused many of her regular customers to return to their homes. It wasn't long after that the Three Trade Horses failed.

"Mary became Mark again, this time as a crewmember of a Dutch merchant ship. And that's how Mary and I met. She was the sailor that spoke English and Dutch on the Dutch merchantman that Jack and I captured."

Annie let out a breath that she wasn't even aware she was holding.

"That is an amazing story, Granny Anne," she said, shaking her head at the tale. "Poor Mary. She had to dress as a man for most of her life. But surely there is more to the story?"

"Yes, Sweet Annie, a lot more. But you will have to wait for that chapter of Mary's life—and mine for that matter. Let's call it a night." Anne was exhausted. Her recent bout with the results of breathing bad air and her bout with the devil that lived in the Kill Devil bottle, she had lost much of her energy. It was up the stairs and back to their bedrooms for the pair.

Sleep came quickly for Anne Cormac. And the morning came even quicker.

Chapter 12

Anne's sleep was restless, filled with dreams about her times with Mary, their frank conversations and their shared experiences of living like a man while being in a woman's body. Visions of close calls of having their masquerade discovered, of celebrated successes and devastating failures.

She dreamed of the time she confided Mary's secret to Calico Jack, and how he had convinced her that sharing him with Mary was the thing to do. In her dreams she recalled that as a good time, though it did create some jealousy between the two women.

There was the joy of being a pirate along side Mary, with the freedom of not having to hide being a woman. But there was also the nauseating stench of that cell the two women had shared. The stench was still fresh in her nostrils as she woke. It was something she had not remembered even once in the 42 intervening years.

Her dreams seemed all too real.

Anne climbed from her bed, walked to the window, slipped open the sash, and took a deep breath of fresh air. This time the familiar decaying marsh odors reminded her of the prison in her dream. She slammed the window shut.

This was a new experience for Anne. The smells of the plantation always reminded her of home. This morning was the first time the smells reminded her of her temporary quarters in Jamaican prison so many years ago.

She paced the room. She cursed the dreams. She lay back on her bed and tightly shut her eyes, but she couldn't erase the images of her dreams. She remembered the Kill Devil bottle. It was the second swallow of the pain medicine that began to numb her brain and made the thoughts of that stinking cell begin to fade. One more swallow and she was able to return to sleep without the dreams.

Morning announced itself with another headache and more questions of what she would tell Annie about her time with Mary and Jack. She had bad memories and another hangover.

Anne returned to the water pitcher and attempted to scrub off the residue of the dream and the Kill Devil. The cool compress eased the pain enough for her to get dressed and moving, but it was the second cup of strong coffee from the kitchen that did the trick.

Leaving the kitchen, she crossed the back yard to the stable where the frisky colt's antics brought a smile to her face. Still, she wondered how she was going to reveal the unorthodox side of her life to Annie.

It wasn't long before Annie joined her at the stableyard. They stood together watching the colt. Anne rested her arm on her granddaughter's shoulder. At some point she hugged the young woman. She slowly turned her head and took stock of her Sweet Annie. The girl was growing into a wise, beautiful woman. A satisfied smile crept across Anne Cormac's face. Annie will be a suitable replacement for her as the mistress of Goose Creek Plantation. Neither of the Cormac women seemed to be in a great hurry to break the spell of this moment. The colt seemed to enjoy having an audience and acted out for his owners.

Anne was the first to break the serenity of this sylvan moment.

"Don't you have chores to do?" It was Anne's parental voice Annie heard. One she knew well.

"I've done most of them, Granny Anne." She paused then added, "I did them before you got up." As the words fell from her lips, the young woman realized she had made a mistake.

"It won't be long before night will be upon us, so get your behind back inside the barn and get to work. There will be no story telling unless all the work around here is done. Oh, and who made you my time keeper?"

Anne did her best to put on her stern face, which was difficult with the remnants of the headache still with her. She knew, too well, that Annie would put off cleaning the stalls until the last moment. She could picture herself doing just that in her early days when she returned to the plantation after her time in that stinking prison. It was the chore that most reminded her of her adventurous life.

Annie knew her grandmother had made an idle threat, but she also knew the importance of her responsibilities. The younger woman ran into the barn, grabbing the pitch fork along the way.

Morning slipped into afternoon into evening with little interaction between the two. Even the evening meal was unusually quiet. Anne still hadn't decided how much more she was willing to say.

The meal ended, signaling the beginning of story time. Anne and Annie maintained their silence even after they had gotten settled in their self-appointed positions. Anne leaned back in the rocking chair and cleared her throat. Her efforts to reposition the frog that occupied it was a waste of time. Her voice cracked slightly as she began.

"I almost feel like I should apologize, Sweet Annie, but truth is truth and that's what I promised you, so here we go." Anne settled in her rocking chair and gently pushed back and forth before beginning.

"You know that Mary and I tried to see if we could have a sexual relationship, and that just didn't work. When I told Jack that Mark was, in truth a *Mary*, he was shocked at first, but it didn't take him long to see the benefits of having another woman on board—at least benefits for him. He told me to sit on the bunk and he started what would be the sales job of his life.

"For all of the right reasons, he said, Mary should move into the captain's quarters with Jack and me. It would be much safer for her, since word was certain to get out and her virtue would be in jeopardy. I started to interrupt him to say she had successfully taken care of herself for many years, why would she be in jeopardy now? But actually, I enjoyed his rationale for having two women in his quarters. 'It just makes sense, good sense,' he continued. 'And she will be good company for you.'

"Yeah, sure. His argument was totally transparent, so I decided to challenge him. 'So,' I asked, 'What's to be our sleeping arrangements?' That was the first time I ever saw Jack at a loss for words. He actually stuttered. 'Well, I... or you... she... well...' So I said, "Couldn't Mary and I just share the cabin with you? We could even swap places, now and then. Wouldn't that work?' I knew that is what he was trying to say, and it actually did make sense to me at the time. I liked Jack but we had no agreement. He had always been a good lover and for a lot of space and security reasons, it was the best use of our resources. And it would be a clear line between us and the crew.

"That afternoon Mary moved into the captain's quarters. We even made a schedule. Every other night he would sleep with one or the other, but he would have one night to himself each week. That was our schedule—except when we were pirating. We each maintained our ship work. And Mary and I both were on the boarding team. We were the best at that job, and it wouldn't give any of the crew members reason to say we were getting special treatment. The amazing thing was that it actually worked.

"On the nights that I was scheduled to be with Jack, Mary would be on watch, and on the nights that Mary was with Jack, I would be on watch. We managed to keep up that schedule for quite a while.

"At sun-up we set sail for the waters around Cuba, a good eight-days journey. The crew could relax. The ship store was fully stocked with enough food and rum for at least a month of adventuring at sea."

Chapter 13

"Well, it didn't take long for us to encounter our first target. We were in the primary channel for Spanish ships carrying sugar from Cuba. We knew that most of the sugar ships were also carrying gold. The Spanish quartermasters thought they were keeping this a secret, but we all knew. There was a galleon riding low in the water, so we knew it was loaded. Sugar wouldn't cause her to ride so low nor move so slow. She was carrying a heavy load.

"We approached her in our normal fashion. Since we had limited heavy cannon power and our intent was to capture not sink, we needed to know how well she was armed. Jack was a good captain, so he maneuvered our sloop just out of normal cannon distance. Six cannon balls fell well short of the target—us. That told us she had at least six cannons. It was several minutes before there was another volley of cannon fire.

"Jack knew that our only chance to capture the galleon was to come alongside while the cannoneers were reloading. It took three rounds of cannon fire for Jack to judge the appropriate lapse of time available for our boarding team to engage the galleon.

"Jack's education and experience proved to be the difference in the strategy we used that day. He turned the sloop and began his run at the galleon at just the right time. Cannonballs fell within three ship's lengths of us, but we were already at top speed as we saw the splashes of all six of the cannon balls. We were alongside before the reloading process was complete. Again, it was Jack's skill in slowing the sloop at just the right moment for us to throw the hooks and bring us to boarding position. We were outnumbered by four-to-one, but no one was a match for us when we were at full strength—and we were that day.

"I boarded with rapier in one hand and pistol in the other, and two more pistols stuffed in my tunic. I shot the first man to charge me and then dodged a cutlass swung by a large, bearded sailor wearing some sort of uniform. The weight of his blade carried him into a vulnerable position. That was my opportunity and I took it, burying the rapier deep into his side. As I pulled my rapier from his lifeless body, I saw Mary with a cutlass in each hand battling two other uniformed sailors. I heard the loud report of a flintlock pistol quickly followed by the whistle of the lead ball traveling way too close to my head for comfort. I turned and snatched one of my other pistols and fired at the sailor who had just fired at me. He was wearing the uniform of a dragoon, characterized by the crossed belts across his chest. My shot hit in the exact center of the cross.

"I watched as if in slow motion as the shot pierced the belt. I saw the look of shock hit his face. As he was falling backward to the deck, I quickly turned to see that Mary had removed the head of one of her challenges and was in the process of removing the sword arm of the other. I also saw a cutlass-wielding sailor headed for her. I drew my third pistol and fired. The shot whistled very close to Mary, but caught the sailor in mid-swing. My shot hit him in his exposed right side. It slowed his swing, and he crumpled to the deck at Mary's feet. She saluted me with her cutlass and returned to the battle, as did I.

"It was unusual to encounter such a ferocious defense of a sugar ship. As I wiped the blood from my rapier, the rest of our crew joined the boarding party. We had lost only one man, while there were 20 bodies dispersed around the deck. Our crew assembled the galleon's crew. Their sailors had lost the desire for battle. They were herded into the bow of the ship as the rest of us searched through the ship's hold. We found a full stock of sugar and 12 chests filled with Mexican gold. We moved the gold and a bit of the sugar to the sloop.

"I caught Mary only moments before she squeezed the trigger of the pistol she was holding to the side of the galleon's captain's head. I reminded her that the captain wasn't the enemy and that we had gotten what we were there for. I had learned enough Spanish to tell him to get on his way and he would still be able to deliver the sugar to his port.

"We headed back to the sloop. As I swung my legs over the side of the galleon, their crew had already begun the task of cleaning the deck. They were tossing bodies overboard left and right. There was a special meal for the sharks that day.

"We had filled the available area for our valuable booty. We had no room for more treasure, so there was no reason to capture another ship. Instead, we set a course for Nassau and Hog Island where we would divide the gold and other treasure. And drink as much of rum as we could.

"It was a short, two-day trip. As Jack maneuvered us toward the place where we were to drop anchor, we saw a small fishing boat that had run aground where we usually entered the island. Jack assigned the boarding team to make the first trip in to the island. Mary and I, along with two more sailors, got in the landing boat and made our way as quickly as possible to find the fishermen. We were ready for anything. We expected these interlopers to be other pirates looking for our treasure buried near the landing place. What we found were three fishermen, thirsty and starving. Even had they been pirates, they would have been no match for the four of us.

"I waved for Jack and the others to come ashore. It was quite a job getting the treasure and rum off-loaded and placed on the island. It was close to sunset when the job was finished. Jack and I brought the fishermen over near the fire. It was clear to us that they were what they said and not what we had feared. Jack gave them a choice. We could kill them on the spot, or they could sign the Articles of Brotherhood and join us, replacing the two members of our crew that were lost in the last battle—not much of a choice for three men stranded on a deserted island with no boat. So we were now at full strength again.

"Jack gathered the crew around the chests of treasure and began dividing it. Once done, the first barrel of rum was brought to the fire. Soon the second followed, then the third. I told Mary we needed to drink sparingly so that we could watch our new sign-ons. I had a strange feeling that they weren't all they said they were.

"Comfortable with the shares of the treasure divided and filled with rum, one after another of our crew passed out. Two of the fishermen had also passed out, but the third continued sipping his rum. I signaled to Mary to lie down, as did I, but I kept one eye on our new pirate. Soon enough he began plundering through at least a dozen of the crew's payment. Oh, he was a smart one, he was. He took a few pieces of gold from each stash—not enough to be missed, but enough to provide himself with a pretty good stash of his own. I decided I would wait until dawn to out this stinking thief.

"Dawn—red, purple, violet, and yellow painted the eastern sky. Slowly the crew began to stir. Our thief was slow to begin his rising routine. He wasn't going to draw any attention to himself. Yes, he was a smart one alright. Finally, everyone was up and Jack suggested that we all make our way to Nassau. It was then that I told Jack that I had something to say to the crew. That was a surprise to Jack, but he agreed readily enough.

"I took my time. First I welcomed the new sign-ons. Then I suggested that they were welcomed additions to our close-knit crew. Then I began talking about the importance of the Articles of Brotherhood and how they were our contract with the captain and with each other. Many of the crew were ready for me to shut up. I looked at the three new men and asked them if they understood how important it was that all crew members followed the Articles in how we were deal with each other. All three said they did. Then I paused, looked right at the offender and said, 'I have personal evidence that one of our new sign-ons has already broken our confederation.' They looked at each other.

"I walked behind them and struck my rapier on the shoulder of the offender. With that, I announced that he had pilfered from his brothers, stolen from their share of the treasure. Two crew members closest to him grabbed him, jerked him up, and pulled knives.

"I said aloud, 'Wait a minute. His crime calls for a judgment by the captain. Captain Jack, what say you?' There was smile that crossed the thief's face. He must have thought Jack would give him leniency.

"Jack waited a few minutes, as if he were thinking it over.

Then he softly said, 'Kill the bastard. We can't have a thief in our small group.'

"Two knives had already been drawn and both were lodged to the hilt in his body. Jack was right. Trust among thieves is essential. His confederates were told to take care of the body.

"Jack knew the importance of trust among his small band and he knew his decision to dispose of a thief would further solidify his band of pirates. There was a lot of hugging and back slapping to show the agreement with the decision. Mary and I got our share of approbation as well, and Jack made a special effort to praise us to the men.

"We stayed at Hog Island two more days working on the boat. Jack was concerned that the boat we were using was too small. He wanted a much larger one—one with a shallow draught that would allow us do our pirating in the many of the region's shallow bays and inlets. Many of Cuba's inlets would not serve galleons and other large ships because they were too shallow. Jack wanted a relatively new ship that had a clean bottom, one with a lot of below deck space for treasure, and one that was both fast and maneuverable. And he wanted a recognizable ship, so, when we stole it, everyone would know that *Calico Jack* Rackham and his pirates were there. He told me he knew of only one ship like he just described—the William.

"The William was a 12-ton, single-masted sloop owned by John Ham. The single mast reduced the weight of the boat, and the design allowed it to carry an extra sail making it one of the fastest boats in the Caribbean. Its deck was 40 feet long and 10 feet wide. The unique design also reduced the depth of the water it could sail in—five feet or so. Its light armament, four carriage guns and two swivel guns also suited Jack since the guns would rarely be used in battles.

"Jack would get a faraway look in his eyes when he talked about the William, but it had never been in Nassau Harbor nor any of the harbors we were in. Jack talked on about where he would go and what he would do if he had the William. I told him that if he was to have the William, providence would put us together. His dream was so far-fetched, I had no idea it would ever happen."

Anne paused, the faraway gleam in her eyes fading into a clear-eyed acceptance of the present day.

"Sweet Annie, one of the lanterns has burned out and the other is burning low. I think it is time to end the story for tonight."

"Don't stop, Granny Anne ," the younger woman said, breathless with excitement! "I can get more oil for the lamps. This is so interesting and I am learning so much about you that I didn't know. Please go on."

"There's always tomorrow, my dear. It's to bed for you... and me."

Anne turned down the lamp and headed to the stairs with her granddaughter. Her concerns about telling her story now seemed unfounded. Sweet Annie was absorbing every word like a new sponge soaks up spilled water.

Anne walked to the open window in her bedroom. A chill wind blew through the lace curtains. The full moon outlined the familiar image before her. She had observed her plantation more times than she could count from that same spot. Always the same, yet always different. She looked up at the moon. There was a large ring around the big lunar face. She spoke aloud the sea captain's saying," Ring around the moon, there's rain here soon."

No one replied so she walked quietly to her bed. Slipping between the fine sheets made her body tingle. Sleep came quickly that night to the mistress of Goose Creek Plantation.

Chapter 14

The sun's intermittent rays made the raindrops on every still thing on Goose Creek Plantation sparkle. It was a happy image for Anne Cormac. All was right with her world. She stretched and scratched her arms and legs. Nothing itched, but it still felt good to scratch.

She slipped on her morning clothes and made her way to Sweet Annie's room. Annie was still asleep, and Anne didn't wake her. The rain would limit morning chores, so Annie could sleep a little longer. The good-morning aroma of freshly made coffee greeted her on her way downstairs. That wonderful smell put a smile on Anne's face and a song in her heart—a confirmation that all was well.

William was there, waiting for her. Was he the harbinger of some problem on the plantation? No, a smile creased his face when he saw Miss Anne enter the room. Anne raised an eyebrow at his presence, then asked the kitchen help to bring coffee and biscuits for her and William. Their conversation was light and positive. The colt was growing. The slave population grew by two, thanks to the full moon births—two healthy, baby boys. The rain would certainly help the corn crop, and the increased humidity would be beneficial to the indigo plants.

As William rose to excuse himself, Annie entered the breakfast room rubbing the night's residue from her eyes and stretching to accompany a big yawn.

Succumbing to the contagious yawn, Anne followed suit with a huge yawn of her own. Annie laughed. "Yawns are catching, aren't they?" she laughed.

Anne laughed in return. "Well, Sweet Annie. How are you this beautiful morning?

"I slept blissfully last evening, Granny Anne . Blissfully. But now I am ready for coffee and a warm biscuit. Do we have any blackberry jelly?"

"You know we always have blackberry jelly. Blackberry brambles are as much a part of Goose Creek Plantation as Spanish Moss and the good old Goose Creek." They both laughed again, enjoying their girlish banter.

Conversation was light as the pair finished breakfast. Annie excused herself to dress for the day, and Anne headed to the barn. She spent some time with the colt and his mother. A group of slave women had gathered in the barn to sing spirituals and shell peas and beans in preparation for drying them for the winter. Anne had learned about the process which had been perfected by the Cherokee Indians in the South Carolina uplands, and introduced it to Goose Creek Plantation.

The practice was started by the Cherokee Indians living around Fort Prince George and their village of Keowee. Anne decided the best way to learn the process was to visit the tribes and see for herself. It was a 12-day trip on horseback, each way. She arrived at the village and asked for a meeting with the chief. Anne was surprised when she found that she would be meeting with another woman and pleased that she would not have to argue with a man.

She was called StillWater. The two women were both strong and decisive, and they recognized that quality in each other. The result was an instant, compatible relationship. Still-Water happily had some of the tribe women show Anne how the process was done. The two women became fast friends. Anne left the village with food and water for the trip home along with the process of drying shelly beans and a promise that StillWater would visit Goose Creek Plantation.

Anne met up with Sweet Annie around midday for a light meal, after which they were joined by William to review the plantation books.

As Anne and Annie adjourned to the veranda, there was a heightened level of excitement in the small talk between the two women. Anne settled in her rocking chair. Annie jumped into the swing. A slight misjudgment almost provided a repeat of her fall. Her actions that followed were much like one of their yard cats when they made a mistake. She looked under the seat like she was looking for something wrong with the swing. Anne smiled.

Once everyone was settled in their proper places, Anne resumed her story.

"Well, let me see. We were still at Hog Island when I left off, and wasn't Jack—yes I remember, Jack was talking about wanting the William.

"As I recall, it was early summer of 1720. I remember that because 1720 was one of the most important years of my adventurous life. When we left Hog Island it was mid-morning. The tide was quite high, and there as a strong westerly wind. Jack announced that we would be heading to the southern tip of Cuba for what he called, easy picking. He didn't want a reprisal of the last visit to Cuba, so he stayed well away from Cienfuegos. It was a 10-day trip from Hog Island to Cuba, and we expected to encounter a few small to medium-sized ships on the way. We did. I don't remember anything special about the encounters, but I remember we had a filled ship store and plenty of rum.

"The next few weeks we traveled south along the Cuban coast. We were near the tip of Cuba when the lookout called that he had spotted a large merchant vessel in the main channel from Hispaniola. Jack said he wanted to watch the ship from afar for the rest of the day. The crew was ready for some action, so playing cat and mouse wasn't what they wanted to hear. I let Jack know that the crew was restless. Jack called us all to the main deck. He explained that he wanted to stay just out of sight of the ship until sunrise. I wasn't happy with Jack's decision. We came very close to a real fight in our cabin. I questioned the quality of his *nutmegs* and called him a dirty *bachelor's son*. He called me a *dirty puzzle* and an *abbess* and said I was acting like a *trot*. I had little to say to him for the rest of the day—but wait, we did.

"As Jack had said, at the first light of day, with sails fully unfurled, we headed for the merchant ship. We approached the port side and fired two cannon balls at the vessel. One ball hit the water near the bow but the other hit the mast that held the mainsail, which covered the main deck with the sail material and virtually disabled the ship. I quickly assembled the boarding crew on our starboard side, ready to board. Board we did.

"A battle followed. I really hadn't expected much of a fight, but we were met by a half-dozen British dragoons, prepared to fight. And a battle it was. Initially there was one of our boarding team battling each of the British troops. We lost one man to a musket ball and another to the cutlass of a well trained swordsman.

"I was wounded—a sword cut on my forearm. It was my left arm. See the scar?"

Anne rolled up her sleeve to reveal the wicked, pale white reminder of her wound, and Annie gasped, half in awe and half in envy.

"I shouted to Mary to hold battle with two dragoons while I tied pieces of the torn sleeve of my shirt around my arm to stop the bleeding. Mary was a fighter, but she was no match for two trained dragoons. She was losing the battle.

"I was able to fire my musket. My target was in the mid-point of a downward slash when my musket ball entered his left side. I'm sure it shattered some ribs, cleared his lung and entered his heart. The look on his face was priceless. He had not expected my shot. His swing hesitated for an instant, then the force of his motion continued the slash. His target, Mary's head, had moved, and he fell face down to the wooden deck of the ship.

"Mary glanced at the lifeless body at her feet. In that moment, the second cutlass wielding dragoon slashed and his sword cut through Mary's shirt and sliced the flesh of her side. It wasn't a mortal wound, but it was enough to take Mary out of the battle. I had already assumed Mary's place in the battle and finished it with a well-done parry and a well-placed thrust.

"There were two dragoons left, though most of the fight had left them. When they surrendered, the ship's captain came to us with a white flag begging for the lives of his men and the safety of his ship. Jack met with him privately and offered safety for his men and ship—if he cooperated with us.

"With that agreement the captain took Jack and I to the ship's hold and showed us the treasure he was carrying. There were two dozen trunks filled with Spanish doubloons. Jack said later that he wondered why there were seasoned British dragoons on a British merchant ship in the waters off Hispaniola. The gold was the reason. The newly minted coins were from Peru and headed to the royal vaults of King George. We deprived old *King Turniphead* of quite a fortune that day.

"King Turniphead, Granny Anne ?" Annie interrupted.

"Yes. Sweet Annie. That is what we called King George, because he was originally from Hanover, Germany. We called him Turniphead because Germany was the source of so many root vegetables—you know beets, potatoes, and turnips."

"Not very respectful, Granny Anne ."

"Most British didn't like the fact that the ruling monarch wasn't from Britain. We Irish just didn't like him, period. In addition to the gold, we got a supply of rum and some food. I was able to flush my wound with rum, and I did the same to Mary's. I then packed the wounds with turmeric we found among the ship's stores to prevent infection."

"Jack called for a vote of the entire crew before deciding the fate to the merchant ship. Mary and I voted to kill the crew and sink the ship. The rest of the crew voted to strip the ship of weapons and leave them with a week's rations. We had already taken their black powder to our magazine, and it was properly stored. The ship had four cannons that we pushed off into the water. The muskets and cutlasses were thrown in the sea. The decision was made to allow them to keep their daggers. When this process was completed our first mate disconnected the ship's rudder. It would take some time to re-connect, and by that time we would be well out of range. With that, Jack bid the captain adieu and we all gathered on deck to salute the other crew.

"We continued our adventurous travels near the southern most point of Cuba in the area where Cuba and Hispaniola are closest. We successfully encountered three more vessels, all small and mostly productive. Our food was running low and so was the rum, so Jack decided it was time to head back to Hog Island and Nassau. We had a favorable wind thanks to the current, so were back in the harbor of Hog Island in six days. We dropped anchor with the sun high overhead. Jack divided the treasure, gave each man a measure of rum, and announced that we were going to Nassau to restock the ship's stores and have a little rest and whiskey, wenches, and widdles.

"In a little over an hour we were entering the Nassau Harbor. Mary, Jack, and I were proudly standing on the bow of the sloop when we entered the harbor. I couldn't believe my eyes and neither could Jack. There, anchored in the middle of the harbor for all to see, was the sleekest ship I had ever seen. The shiny black hull almost glowed in the evening sun. The long, pointed bowsprit looked like an arrow poised of a fully cocked bow ready to do battle.

"The William. The ship of Jack's dreams was right here within his reach—right here in the Nassau Harbor! We anchored across the harbor from the William—a place where Jack could watch the comings and goings from the ship, but not close enough for anyone to see him watching.

"When we left the ship, we went to Jack's house. Mary was with us. That evening we ate at one of the nicer restaurants. There in one of the corners was John Ham and his entourage. He was nothing like I expected. I had imagined him bigger-than-life, a giant among mortal men. In reality he was short and fat, red-faced from too many nights spent drinking rum.

Regardless of how different he was from my image, there he was in all of his glory. Mary, Jack and I spent much of the evening observing the infamous John Ham.

"Ham, we knew, was from a wealthy family in Spain. He acquired one of the large plantations on Barbados and started growing sugar cane. He obtained more and more land, and soon was the largest sugar cane farmer on the island. His sugar processing factory made him the richest man in Barbados, by far. It was rare for him to be in Nassau, since the trip from Barbados took nearly a month. I noticed that I knew a couple of the men with him from my days at Pierre's coffee. I decided I would visit my friend Pierre, the Pansy Pirate, and see what I could find out. We waited for Ham and his party to leave before we left for Jack's house.

"I was at Pierre's Coffee shop early the next morning. It was good to see my friend again. When I walked in the shop, I noticed a chair hanging on the wall like a piece of sculpture or wall art. There was a small sign next to it—"Anne's Chair." Then I remembered that Maria Renaldi was sitting in a chair like it when I met Chidley Bayard. I asked Pierre about it."

"'Remember when you were challenged by Maria for taking her man?' Pierre said. 'She took one swing at you with a borrowed cutlass, then you did away with her with one thrust of your rapier. So, that's Anne's Chair.' Pierre has such a sense of humor. I asked him why. 'Why, I just had to do it,' he replied, as if it were the most obvious thing in the world. 'It was the first killing that took place in this establishment.' But not the last, I'm sure.

"Well, Pierre bought me a cup of coffee, and poured himself a cup of English breakfast tea. We started with some small talk—you know, about the pirates we knew, mostly who's alive and who's dead. Finally he asked me, 'Anne, you have never come slumming in my part of Nassau unless you needed some advice or wanted some information. Which is it?'

"I laughed at him, but I knew he was right. I told him of our idea to steal the William right under Ham's nose. He was absolutely giddy. I knew he would be. I asked him what he knew about the ship and their plans. He said if we actually planned to steal the ship we would have to move fast, because they planned to leave Nassau in two days. He said we were in luck because he knew of plans to have a party away from the ship the very next evening, and that there would only be a crew of three left to secure the ship. He said he personally knew two of the three chosen, and they wouldn't represent much of a fight.

"He filled in some more blanks about the layout of the ship. I thanked him and headed to Jack's house.

"I interrupted Jack and Mary occupying their time while I was away. Having time alone resulted in only one activity. I grabbed the coverlet and yanked it as I yelled at them. 'Get up and git your clothes on. We have a lot to do and little time to do it.' Mary grabbed her musket and Jack, his dagger. In Nassau, you never did anything without a weapon nearby. When they saw it was me they both started cursing. I told them to shut up and get dressed."

"'What are you talking about?' Jack demanded, and at the same time Mary declared, 'I'll get even with you for interrupting my pleasuring.'

"I answered Mary first, 'You cheap bitch, we aren't anywhere close in being even in the interrupting category.' Without so much as taking a breath I fixed Jack with a withering glare and said, 'I'm about to fulfill your greatest desire.'

"'I was already doing that, when you barged in,' Mary sulked.

"'Oh, shut up, woman,' I spat back. 'You're nowhere close in that category either. Now, both of you, quit your yammering. We need to talk about the William.'

"As I filled them in on my conversation with Pierre, a plan started to take shape. Jack had to assemble a crew suitable for manning the William. I had to gather sufficient ship's stores to augment what was already on the ship. And Mary had to acquire enough black powder to handle the six canons and all of our muskets. It was good there were three of us.

"Everything was ready at dusk the next evening. Jack had found a dozen men he felt he could trust. I had found a large row boat that would hold the crew, food, and black powder. An hour after dusk we silently rowed out to where the William was anchored. A hanging ladder was right where we needed it. Obviously, the small crew didn't expect that anyone would be bold enough to board the ship.

"We split into two groups, each group moving with clandestine silence, moved from the stern where we found the ladder to the bow. We found the crew. One was asleep, the other two were drinking rum. There was no battle. They quickly surrendered. We checked out each of our positions and found the William ready to meet our needs. Jack sent the crew down the ladder and into the row boat. It would take them some time to get through the harbor and to the place where the party was still going on. I would have loved to have been there when the three told Ham that his pride and joy had been stolen.

"It was dark and rainy. Luck was with us. We slipped by the Harbor Guard and were well out of the Nassau harbor when the sun hit the horizon.

"For the next couple of weeks we slipped in and out of the islands of the Bahamas. We encountered a few ships and looted what we could, but we didn't get much of value.

"One of the ships we robbed was owned by James Gohier. Gohier was a friend of Governor Woodes Rogers. It was Rogers that had forbidden Jack and me from being together. Gohier reported our piracy to the Governor, and Rogers immediately dispatched a sloop fully armed with 45 men on board to find us and bring Jack and me to him. But, that didn't happen."

Anne was overcome by a coughing fit. Annie jumped off the swing and hurried to her grandmother's side. She held up her hand to let the young woman know she was OK, but when she stopped coughing, her voice was clearly strained.

"It's alright, Sweet Annie." She paused to catch her breath. "I'm OK." Another pause. "But I think that was a sure sign that it is time to stop our storytelling session until tomorrow."

Annie helped the older woman up just as another coughing jag started. Slowly the pair made it to the stairs and to their respective bedrooms.

"Are you sure you are alright, Granny Anne ?" Annie asked from the door to her room.

"Yes. I think I just talked a little too long. Sleep well, Sweet Annie."

For once sleep came quickly for Anne. The story telling had taken a great deal of energy. The bedroom window stayed closed and that silenced the singing from the slave quarters. Anne slept all night. But, her dreams were of those pirate days.

Chapter 15

When Anne awoke the sun was streaming in her bedroom window. The warm, bright light made the room look and feel happy. It was a happiness that spread like a big duck-down comforter over the entire room. The warm happiness spread to Anne as well. It even warmed the chill that the dreams of her harsh buccaneering days had left in her memory. It was a new day. A day that started warm and happy.

The warmth and happiness was catching, and everyone on the plantation caught what the sun was spreading around. Smiles were everywhere, and there were even happy songs rising from the slave quarters and from those working in the fields. It was, indeed, a happy day.

Annie asked her grandmother at least four times if the story of the William would continue after the evening meal. She was obviously enthralled by her grandmother's story. Amused, Anne said nothing, but only allowed a sly smile to turn up the corners of her mouth.

At last the meal ended—not soon enough for Annie, but ended nonetheless.

The sun settled low on the horizon, and the sky was beginning to darken as the pair reclaimed their seats. William brought lighted lamps, assuming there would be a need for such light before the evening would end. Tea was served—a pleasantry for Anne, and a somewhat annoyance to the young girl who was ready to get on with the story. At length Anne decided she had playfully tormented her granddaughter long enough.

"The William turned out to be everything we expected and more. It was fast. Even fully loaded, it could easily outrun any ship that we might encounter. It was maneuverable and stable, even in tight turns. We were ready to have some fun—and to get rich.

"As I said, we were pirating the ships we encountered in the southern waters of the Bahamas. Two of those ship's captains informed us that Governor Rogers had dispatched the sloop with orders to take us, and that a substantial bounty was being offered for our capture. In addition to the bounty, Rogers was offering an extra 50 pieces of gold to the captain and 10 pieces of gold to every crew member if Jack, Mary, and I were captured alive and the ship was returned intact. We considered that high praise.

"Since one of the captains said Governor Rogers had sent the ship south in hopes of finding us, we changed our course and headed to Berry Island. As we approached Berry we met a sloop that looked like it was riding deep, indicating it was carrying a heavy cargo. We took it with no resistance and found that it was carrying a load of gold headed for New Providence and then to Cienfuegos, Cuba, to buy sugar. It was our first big haul since acquiring the William, and as such it was a reason to celebrate. Celebrate, we did.

"We didn't know it at the time, but that ship's captain continued his trip, minus the gold, to New Providence Island and Nassau, and immediately reported our piracy to Governor Rogers. That was September 2nd. Rogers dispatched another ship after us, and two days later, September 4th, Rogers issued a proclamation:"

Jack Rackham and his crew swear destruction on all those who belong to the Island of New Providence

"That officially branded us, and made us a target for any ship from Nassau.

"When we heard that, Jack set sail for Hispaniola even though we were sailing against the wind and current. It took us four weeks. On October 1st, we captured two English merchant sloops. We took very little of value, but we were able to refill our ship's store. That was good because we were running low on food and rum.

"On October 10th, we saw a Spanish galleon running slow and deep, obviously loaded with heavy cargo, probably gold from Jamaica headed to Spain. We first experienced cannon fire before we were in cannon range. That usually meant they were trying to scare us. Jack maneuvered the William skillfully. First on the port side of the galleon, then he would cross over to the starboard side staying just out of reach of the cannon fire.

"Volley after volley were fired by the galleon's cannoneers. All missed their mark. Soon the cannons were quiet. Carefully, Jack guided the William to the port side of the galleon just out of musket range. We were close enough for a good cannon shot but the lack of cannon fire indicated they had exhausted their supply of cannonballs. Jack called for one cannon shot aimed at the main mast. Our cannoneer was an expert at placing cannonballs on target.

"Shortly after our first shot, I saw the main mast fall. We cheered the direct hit. With the loss of support, the main sails fluttered down covering much of the deck. Jack called for the boarding team to the starboard side as he guided the William alongside the galleon. We quickly boarded the ship and a fierce battle ensued. When the captain finally displayed the white flag there were 26 bodies on the deck. Five were our men.

"The ship was loaded with gold and sugar. We took all of the gold and some of the sugar along with 15 barrels of rum, leaving them with one barrel. Since they had lost well over half of their able men and had no main sail they represented little threat to us. Jack decided not to sink the ship. Four of their able men agreed to sign on with us, so we ended that adventure only one man short.

"We continued on our trip past Hispaniola headed to Jamaica, away from the ships looking for us. It was October 16th, I think, when our luck started turning. We were near Porto Maria Bay, Jamaica, when we encountered the Neptune, a small merchant vessel out of Port Royal, Jamaica. We gained its surrender with only musket fire. We took 50 rolls of tobacco, nine bags of allspice, and some other salable staples. Jack forced the captain of the Neptune to follow us under the threat that we would use our superior cannon power to sink the ship if he refused.

"We continued west along the coast of Jamaica. The next day we encountered the Mary and Sarah, another small merchant sloop. We took it with little resistance, and since it was new, Jack said we could get good money for it. He forced them to follow us as well. We were now a flotilla of three ships, and Jack soon realized that we could not manage all three. On the 19th of October, he allowed the captain of the Neptune to go his own way.

"Managing those two additional ships slowed our progress.

We had barely reached Negril Point, the western most point of Jamaica. .By the 20th, Jack decided to release the Mary and Sarah as well. Now we were back to just one ship, the William. That was something for the crew to celebrate, so Jack maneuvered the sloop into a safe, small harbor, dropped anchor, and ordered two barrels of rum brought to the deck. I questioned Jack, but I was told that the crew needed a little break and an afternoon of drinking would do them good. Jack's decision was our undoing.

"Sometime around 10 o'clock on the evening of the 20th of October, the Snow-Tyger commanded by Captain Jonathan Barnet discovered us at anchor in Dry Harbor Bay. The crew had been drinking most of the day and none were suitable to defend the ship. Most were already passed out below deck. I saw that Barnet was flying the Union Jack, so I ordered one of the crew to raise the British flag. Captain Barnet yelled for us to identify our ship and Captain. Jack yelled back, 'Captain John Rackham from Cuba.' Then Barnet ordered us to surrender. Jack's answer was to order our cannoneer to fire the swivel gun at Barnet's ship. It was dark and the cannoneer was drunk. His shots didn't even come near the Snow-Tyger. I grabbed my musket and fired, but Barnet was out of range. My guess is that our fire just made Barnet mad. His cannoneer fired only once. The shot hit our main mast, rendering escape impossible.

"Barnet maneuvered his ship close to board the William. When the drunken crew saw that, they scrambled below deck—for what reason, I have no idea. Jack joined them. That left me and Mary on deck to defend the William.

"At least 40 of Barnet's men jumped aboard the William. I called to the men to come up and fight like men. None came.

Mary and I fought valiantly, but as you might imagine, we were outnumbered, outgunned, and quickly overwhelmed. Truth be told, we should have lost our lives then and there, but Governor Rogers' offer of extra gold if we were brought back alive was certainly reason enough for us to be captured and not killed.

"I have never in my life surrendered—and I didn't that day—but Mary and I were nonetheless overpowered. Barnet's men stormed the area below deck where the crew was hiding. They were all captured along with the drunken Jack Rackham. As they were herded aboard the Snow-Tyger, Jack looked at me and said, 'What could I do?'

"I lost all respect for John *Calico Jack* Rackham. I sneered at him and said, 'If you had fought like a man instead of hiding, you wouldn't have to die like the dirty dog you are.' Then I spit at him.

"I only saw Jack one more time—when we were offloaded in Port Royal where we were all imprisoned. I never spoke to him again.

"Mary and I were in one cell. Jack, George Featherstone, and Richard Corner were together in another cell, and the rest of the crew were in one larger cell. At least Mary and I had a little privacy. Our cell was small, and the drainage was poor, so the floors were muddy. Our food, if you could call it that, was overcooked cassava. Once a week we would get salted dried meat. The cassava looked like potato mush, but had no taste. Because there were no facilities for disposing of human waste in the cell, it smelled like a dog kennel. We heard cries and shouts coming from the direction of where the crew was being kept. At the trials we noticed that many of them had been seriously mistreated. Some had unset broken bones making them appear horribly deformed. Two had lost ears, and others had been branded.

"I overheard the guards talking that the local governor, Nicholas Lawes, was taking particular interest in these trials and the prisoners. Then I remembered that it was his sister that I had punched at Chidley's party. Oh well.

"We were being held in the prison in Port Royal, but the trials were to be held in Admiralty High Court in Saint Jago de la Vega. The first trial was November 16th. Mary and I, along with the entire crew, were herded into the crowded court room. We were all in chains, facing an ominous group of men dressed in black robes.

"I knew there was no possibility of leniency when I saw the Governor himself, Nicholas Lawes, presiding over the court. Most of the crew were tried and found guilty, then hanged the next day in the public square for all the citizens to see.

"On November 17th, Jack and the ship's officers were found guilty and sentenced to be hanged. We were sent back to prison. The next day, November 18th, Jack, George Featherstone, Richard Corner, John Davies, and John Howell were taken to Port Royal to be hanged at Gallows Point to accommodate the larger crowd that assembled to watch the execution.

"It was Sunday morning. As a part of the spectacle, a pig cart was chosen to carry Jack, Featherstone, Corner, Davies, and Howell to Gallows Point. It was driven by Kingston Parish Church and almost the entire congregation followed joining dozens of others taking part in the festivities surrounding the hanging of the famous pirates. Public hangings were always social events, but Lawes was going out of his way to make this one extra special. The governor furnished food and rum to all who turned out to be certain that there was a big crowd.

"He and the other members of the Admiralty Court wore their black robes. His sister was there, dressed as if the execution was one her celebrity balls. The pirates had been condemned by Governor/Judge Lawes as evil with no redeeming qualities and being in league with the Devil, himself. As such, although the rector of the parish was there, there were no last rites for the condemned men.

"I am told the festivities were loud and boisterous, but there was a moment of silence when the executioner climbed the steps to carry out the hangings. As the five men fell the short space to stretch the ropes, the cheering and shouting started again. The partying lasted long after the last of the involuntary jerks of the hanged had stopped.

"I was told that Jack was *gibbeted* at Plumb Point. His body was tied in a metal harness, a gibbet, on a post for public viewing. Plumb Point was a sandy point at the entrance to Port Royal Harbor, so every ship had to pass the rotting body of John *Calico Jack* Rackham. Featherstone and Corner were *gibbeted* at Bush Key and Gun Key respectively. Governor Lawes issued a proclamation that piracy would no longer be overlooked in Jamaica. I expect he was looking forward to putting me there as well. I'm sure his sister was.

"Nine days later, Mary and I were marched back into the court room to face Governor Lawes and the Admiralty Court. Lawes was grinning as we entered the court room. And there was his fat, ugly, snaggletoothed sister. She was grinning too. I spat at her when we passed her. I knew I was doomed so what difference did it make.

"Lawes called the proceedings to order and the Court

Register introduced us to the court and read our charges. I remember his statement like it was yesterday.

"Honorable Lord Governor Nicholas Lawes, and distinguished counselors and commissioners of the High Court of the Admiralty. Today approach Mary Reid and Anne Bonny, late of the Island of New Providence, Spinsters, charged with Piracies, Felonies and Robberies on the High Sea.'

"I suppose he thought we were never married. He was interrupted by noise in the court room. 'Hang them!' was yelled from all corners of the room. He quieted the crowd and proceeded with the charges.

"'These women did, on numerous occasions, feloniously and wickedly rob and plunder ships on the High Seas. They did...'

"Before he could finish he was interrupted by Governor Lawes. 'I think we have heard enough.' He looked directly and me and said, 'How do you plead?' Together we said 'Not guilty.' Again the court proceedings were interrupted by shouts from the court room.

"Court began. We were required to sit through graphic descriptions of the things we were accused of doing. Finally, Lawes held his hand up. The court was silent. He motioned the assembled judges. They formed a small circle. I heard the word, 'Guilty.' They assumed their seats and there was a moment of silence. Lawes cleared his throat and in a most distinguished voice announced:

"'Mary Reid and Anne Bonny, you have been found guilty of Piracy, Felonies and Robbery on the High Sea, each of these charges carry the sentence of hanging by the neck until dead.'

"He was interrupted by cheering. Again his raised hand resulted in silence.

"'On tomorrow, you will be carried to Gallows Point where

your sentence will be carried out. Do you have anything to say to this court?'

"I stood and Mary stood with me. 'Lord, we plead our bellies.'

"There was a moment of silence and pandemonium broke out. Mary and I were both pregnant, carrying Jack Rackham's babies. Since unborn babes were considered innocent, it was unlawful to hang a pregnant woman. Everyone there knew the court could not hang a pregnant woman. There was nothing more he could do.

"The people who had come to see the spectacle were disappointed and angry. The Governor picked up a musket just in case someone tried to charge the table that separated the court and judges from the spectators. I think the people were more mad at the Governor and judges than they were at Mary and me. The one making the most noise was the fat, ugly sister of Governor Lawes. She jumped up and lunged at me. I raised my elbow just in time to catch her jaw. The full force of that fat pig's lunge drove my elbow into her jaw. I heard the cracking of bones above the noise in the court room. I smiled, even in my desperate situation, knowing that she would have many months of recovery and possibly, never talk again.

"So Mary and I went back to prison."

Chapter 16

"Sweet Annie, I need to take a break. This was a very traumatic time in my life, and reliving it has left me exhausted."

The older woman started to stand but fell back into her chair. Her granddaughter rushed to the rocking chair to help, but Anne had already regained her composure and was in the process of standing.

"Let's go inside, Granny Anne. We can pick up the story tomorrow, or later if you need to."

Back in her room, Anne Cormac removed her clothes and climbed into her bed. Moments later she was deep in sleep. She barely stirred until 11 o'clock the next morning. There was no need for the chamber pot during the night, and she didn't even change positions. The sleep was refreshing, dream-free night.

Normal morning activities at the plantation went on as if she were there to direct them. She enjoyed lunch with her granddaughter and together they walked to the barn where the warm sun helped invigorate the older woman and seeing the frisky colt made her happy. She was alive and the residue from last evening's storytelling had been washed away, left in the bowl and pitcher in the bedroom.

They spent the rest of the day together. It was a happy time, something Anne desperately needed. With their evening meal finished, Anne and Annie ended up on the veranda in their accustomed seats, and Anne prepared to resume her tale.

"Well, Sweet Annie, I suppose you could say I had reached the low point in my life. Mary and I had been convicted and sentenced to hang, but we had a short reprieve—at least until our babies were born. Then they would hang us. All we could do was sit and wait to die.

"We still shared that same tiny cell, and because of the near constant rain—Jamaica's rainy season is usually over in October but here it was late November and it was raining almost every day—we didn't get out very often. Tradition dictated that prisoners were to be allowed out of the cell once a day, but that just didn't happen. Women in Jamaican prisons were usually dirty puzzles, and they were used by all of the guards. But Jamaica's Catholic heritage played to our favor, and since we were pregnant, we were left alone.

"We spent the many hours together, Mary and I, talking, waiting for our daily crust of bread and the bucket of water from which we drank and washed ourselves. Those days in prison were a special form of hell. The days dragged into weeks. We lost track of time.

"One morning, perhaps a month later, I honestly don't know how long, I awoke to hear Mary sobbing. She was trembling, her body wracked with fever, her face contorted by the pain, her eyes open, eyeballs bugging out of their sockets. Her mouth, slack-jawed in her effort to force more air into her lungs, all gave her an otherworldly look. Her last words were, 'Don't let the bastards win. I love you.' She loudly exhaled and was still.

"I knew she was dead. Her babe twisted and turned in her belly for what was probably only a few moments but seemed like an hour, then it was still, too.

"When the guard came to check on us I told him Mary was

dead. He called another guard and they dragged her body out of the cell by her ankles. I hope they gave her a proper burial. She was a good woman and a good pirate. But based on the way they took her from the jail cell—no ceremony, no respect—I doubt she gained respect in burial. No respect in life, no respect in death."

Anne's gaze took on a faraway look, and her voice grew pensive.

"Day—Night—Day—Night—Day—Night. I lost count. What did I care? What did I have to live for? The cell was barely livable with Mary there. With her gone, one bad day followed another. The damp cell seemed damper. The stinking cell seemed to smell worse. And the days were endless, and the nights were worse. The seemingly endless moving of the baby in my belly served only to remind me that I had nothing to live for. As soon as it was born I would hang. I would not be allowed to hold my baby, never suckle it—never see it grow.

"Without Mary, my misery quickly turned to despair and my despair to depression. I would cry for no reason—well, no specific reason. Then I would catch myself and begin a conversation with myself. *Here you are, Anne Bonny, one of the most feared pirates alive, crying like a little girl.*

"Upon a day the jailer brought me two crusts of bread. He didn't say why, and I didn't ask. The extra bread would be good for my baby. The extra bread went on for three or four days. Then, he brought me two buckets of water and a rag. He said to clean up because I had a visitor and that I should look presentable. I had to laugh. I was filthy and my cloths were mostly threads. And who could be visiting me? I didn't know many people in Jamaica. Could it be that snaggletooth bitch daughter of the Governor who put me in this prison? I didn't think so. But I was grateful for the extra water.

"That afternoon, I was courteously escorted to the office of the jailer. There, with a big smile on his face, was Pierre. He was the last person I expected to see. He had some clean clothes in a valise. He hugged me, then crinkled his nose and whispered in my ear, 'You need a bath, girl.'

"To my complete and utter amazement, the jailer presented me with a pardon, signed by the Governor. Pierre escorted me out to a carriage and off we went to Port Royal where a sloop was waiting. We got on board and Pierre told the cabin boy to take me to my cabin and make sure there was enough water for me to clean myself up. To me Pierre said, 'Get cleaned up, put on some scent, and I have some nice clothes for you there as well. When you are comfortable, I will tell you the whole story.'

"I bathed and dressed, then met Pierre on deck. He had set up a place for us to talk just outside the captain's quarters. He had mugs of grog, some fresh fruit he had obtained while he was in Port Royal, and some salmagundi. He sat silently, allowing me to eat and drink until I was sated, then I asked the obvious question.

"He told me that my father contacted him shortly after he learned that I had been sentenced to hang and that I was pregnant. He asked Pierre to meet with the Governor to discuss what it would take to buy my freedom.

"Initially the Governor wasn't interested in discussing any terms that would keep me from the gallows. After all, on two occasions I had embarrassed his sister, possibly leaving her speechless with the last one. Two things were in my favor however. First, my father told him to negotiate my release regardless of the cost. Second, my father owned or controlled most of the factors in the Port of Charles Town. He suggested that if the Governor wasn't interested in the money, he should consider that Mister Cormac had the power and influence to initiate an informal blockade of Jamaica. Pierre said that when he mentioned the blockade, the Governor's interest changed and a release was agreed on.

"The trip to Charles Town took five days. With the addition of good food and fresh water to my diet, the life within my belly was much more active. The trip gave me the opportunity to sleep soundly and for Pierre and I to talk more about old times and mutual friends in Nassau. When I told him about the latest encounter with Governor Lawes' sister, he burst out laughing. He was almost as gleeful about the broken jaw as he was about the idea of our first pirate adventure.

"We arrived in Charles Town, but the sloop didn't stop at the port, nor at the warehouses where cargo was offloaded, and not at the slaver dock where many thousands of slaves had been brought to work on the multitude of plantations that now populated the region surrounding Charles Town. Instead, the sloop sailed, silently up Goose Creek until it reached a single docking point and the southern most point of Goose Creek Plantation. Within moments my father was there with a buggy to carry me to the plantation house.

"Only William was here to greet me and escort me to my former room. William informed me that the agreement my father had made with the Governor of Jamaica had not been discussed among the plantation staff, and that I would be there only one day before being transported to the up-country Mulberry Plantation where my father had made arrangements for my care with an old family friend.

I would be there so that I could regain my strength and birth my baby.

"William said my father would accompany me on the trip. He also told me that he understood that I would return to Goose Creek Plantation and, if I wished, would take over running the plantation for my father.

"William led me to my room. It was much as I remembered it. He told me that he would attend to my needs, since none of the house staff was to know I was there.

"I was at the plantation for two nights. My meals were served in my room. On the second morning my father and I were in a comfortable carriage that was joined by a wagon carrying my clothes and previsions for us, two drivers, our most experienced birthing slave, and two men who would see to our safety on the two-day journey to Mulberry Plantation, which was owned by our family friend Thomas Broughton. I was to be the guest of the Broughton's until the baby was born and I was fully recuperated from the birth.

"In the meantime he released the information that I was soon to return from my extended visit to Boston. That information spread through Charles Town like wildfire. I know there was a lot of speculation about how true the story was, but no one would dare challenge my father or his story.

"Your mother was born with very little effort, and, in a short time I had recovered from both the birth and from my ordeal in the Jamaican prison."

Exhausted from reliving her death sentence and subsequent salvation, Anne sank back in her rocking chair, closed her eyes, and breathed deep the familiar scents of the plantation. A small smile turned the corners of her mouth and she declared, "Sweet Annie, I think it is time for me to go upstairs. I will pick up the story and what my father told me about my release when we talk again tomorrow night."

As they had for many nights, Anne and Annie climbed the stairs hand in hand.

Anne sat by the window. Though weary, she wasn't quite ready for sleep. She gazed at the stars, thinking back to the many nights she had spent on decks of a variety of pirate boats looking at these very same stars. They helped her forget the bad days. They were there to soothe the disappointment of her time with James Bonny. They shared her happiness in meeting Jack and Mary and all their successful pirate adventures. They were there when she was in the Jamaican prison. They would look in on her most nights through the little window at the back of her cell. Even on cloudy nights, she knew they were there, and that comforted her. In prison, she would long for night time so she could see the stars. They were the one thing that kept her sane after Mary's death.

The soft, tropical smell of gardenias wafted on the breeze, as did the acrid smell of the smoldering fires from the slave quarters. And, the smell of the marsh—the smells of home. Telling her story to her granddaughter had been cathartic— something she hadn't expected.

Tomorrow night's storytime would start the story of the beginning of her new life—a life with one foot in the past and one in the present.

Chapter 17

After breakfast, Anne asked William to have the horses saddled for Annie and her. A ride would be a good excuse to show Annie the extent of the plantation she would own one day. They rode north to where Foster's Creek flowed into Goose Creek. Foster's creek was the northern boundary of the plantation. Then they road south to where Goose Creek joined the Cooper River and down to the dock where the sloop from Jamaica was met by Anne's father—the southern boundary of the plantation.

Anne dismounted, indicating they were going to stay for a while. Annie also dismounted. They tied the horses and walked out onto the dock. They sat on the end of the dock that had so many times been the departure and entry point for Anne Cormac, Charles Town Socialite and plantation owner—and occasionally, Anne Bonny, part-time pirate. They sat quietly, lost in thought. It was Annie who broke the silence.

"I really love this place." She was speaking to herself more than to her grandmother.

"Remember this moment, Sweet Annie. It will comfort you when running this plantation gets to be difficult. And mark me, it will get difficult. That love is what got me through many hard times." The older woman swallowed a knot in her throat, looked sideways at Annie, and said again more softly in a voice tinged with emotion, "Remember this moment and that love." She almost started crying.

The moment passed, and at last the pair got back in the saddle and rode back to the plantation. It was a perfect day for a silent ride. Birds serenaded them the entire ride. Occasionally, a cricket would chime in. Deer and squirrels came out to watch the riders. A flock of geese flew over in their trademark V formation, honking their song. When the pair stopped to rest the horses in a grass-filled meadow, a warren of rabbits hopped nearby. Two of the kits got close enough to see the humans sitting on the grass before the buck herded them back to the group.

They crossed a stream. Anne noticed a beaver building a dam—soon a home for his family. A badger was standing beside the stream as if he was waiting for the amphibious creatures that would be drawn to the resulting pond.

The horses picked up the pace as they neared the plantation. It was as if they knew they were nearing food and a resting place.

"See you at dinner," was Anne's only words. It had been an inward day for Anne Cormac—a thinking day. Much of her thoughts were centered on Annie's mother. Anne named her baby girl Mary to honor both her mother, Mary Brennen, and her pirating sidekick, Mary Reid.

Interlude

SOME OF THE BACK STORY

Mary Cormac was like her mother Anne in every way. She looked like her mother—fiery red hair and emerald green eyes—and she had her mother's Irish temper. As a young child she was always into trouble. And, like her mother, the only one who could really handle her was her Papa, Anne's father.

Young Mary was into everything. She would throw an animated tantrum anytime she didn't get what she wanted. Anne couldn't deal with her and had three servants whose only job was to keep Mary safe and out of trouble. It was all the three servants could do to keep up with her, much less keep her out of trouble. By the time she was 12, every nanny and private tutor in the state of South Carolina had been employed and had quit, most in tears including the male tutors.

When Mary was 13, Anne hired a handsome young man to be Mary's tutor. Pierre had recommended him and assured Anne his preference was young boys. Anne told Pierre that if anything happened between the tutor and Mary that she would have *two* pairs of nutmegs hanging on the wall of her bedroom—the tutor's and Pierre's.

Mary and Anne went by carriage to meet this new tutor

as he got off the boat from London. Patrick-Martin, a well-dressed young man, was among the first getting off the boat, indicating he was traveling first class. Certainly, a gesture from Pierre. His navy blue jacket and navy and yellow ascot suggested an education at The King's Hospital, the common name of The Hospital and Free School of King Charles II, Ireland's oldest school in Dublin. The Blue Coat school—named after the uniform all students wore—was a coeducational boarding school of the Church of Ireland.

Patrick-Martin walked smartly down the boarding plank to the captain, nodded and asked the whereabouts of Miss Anne Cormac. The Cormac carriage was pointed out and the young Irishman headed toward Anne's carriage. He approached Anne and announced himself.

"Miss Anne Cormac, Patrick-Martin Doyle, at your service." He bowed at the announcement of his name. "I understand you are in need of a tutor. I am a graduate of King's Hospital in Dublin and a recent graduate of Cambridge University. My sponsor, a well-positioned gentleman in Nassau, has employed me and given me clear and absolute instructions. I believe I am up to your needs."

"We'll see," Anne said. "Yes, we shall see."

For the next two years, Mary was a different girl. She was attentive to her class work. She became a proficient horse-woman. She excelled in mathematics and was soon working with her grandfather on the plantation books. The remarkable change in her demeanor was all attributed to Patrick-Martin.

Mary's face brightened when Patrick-Martin entered the room. Indeed, she exhibited all of the outward expressions of puppy love. Anne watched Patrick-Martin carefully, but found no evidence that the infatuation was, in any way, mutual.

As the end of the second year of Patrick-Martin's contracts, he made it known that he would be leaving and going to Nassau. With that announcement, Mary reverted back to her previous nature. No one could control her. She was, in a word, a hellion.

At her wit's end, Anne consulted with her father, and together they decided to send Mary to King's Hospital School. Mr. Cormac sent four servants to accompany his granddaughter—two men and two women. Once she finished school she was to return to Goose Creek Plantation.

Mary was 15 when she left for Dublin, Ireland. The spirited young girl had high hopes of finding another Patrick-Martin.

Peace and quiet returned to Goose Creek Plantation—for a season.

It was a cold winter. William Cormac insisted on being at his office everyday except Sunday. It was Tuesday, thus Cormac prepared to go to his office. Frost covered everything so heavily that it looked like snow in some places. The patron of Goose Creek, dressed in as many coats and scarves as he could stand to wear, began his carriage ride into Charles Town. It was the beginning of a normal day.

In less than an hour, a messenger from a neighboring plantation arrived at the Goose Creek Plantation house. Master Cormac had been discovered beneath his overturned carriage. William, Cormac's longtime steward, went immediately to the scene of the accident. There was no sign of any problem and no evidence that Master Cormac had struggled.

William quickly returned to the Goose Creek Plantation house and informed Anne about her father's condition. They prepared another carriage for travel, gathering some men from the fields to assist. By the time Anne arrived it was clear that the most powerful man in Charles Town was dead.

Anne was devastated. This foreign land, now her home, had taken the two people who were her life, her mother and now her father. She was alone.

The servants righted the carriage. William gathered the papers that were scattered around the scene and placed William Cormac's body in the carriage that he and Anne shared. Anne wept opening and unashamed. Just outside the entrance to Goose Creek Plantation, William halted the carriage. He knew Anne was crushed by her father's death, but he also knew that she was now in charge of the vast estate. She needed to display the appearance of being in control, even when she wasn't. The two sat in silence for a few moments, then William gave her the advice she would need as the new Mistress of Goose Creek Plantation.

The plantation and all of William Cormac's diverse businesses were all on her shoulders. So were the lives of all of the slaves at Goose Creek Plantation. Each of the farm slaves, each of the house slaves, each of the maintenance slaves, all the hired hands and company employees—they would all be looking to her for support and their livelihood. It was imperative that she appear strong and in charge. She must deal with her grief in private.

William assured her that he would always be there to provide advice. Even in her grief, Anne understood what William was telling her.

Two days later, the preacher of the AnaBaptist church along with dozens of families in carriages lined the road to Goose Creek Plantation to participate in the burial ceremonies. Cormac's trusted steward William was there with all of the Cormac slaves and house servants. William Cormac was buried next to the love of his life, Mary Brennan, on the property that had symbolized his life in Charles Town and in America.

Many people owed a lot to William Cormac. But as Anne would soon discover, William Cormac owed a lot to people in Charles Town.

Now, back to our story.

Chapter 18

"Well, Sweet Annie, our ride today brought back many memories. Memories of your mother. I haven't heard from her in 17 years." Her voice dropped to a low whisper. "And the happy memories of you growing up. You have been the delight of my life, child. Memories of your grandfather and his death, and the troubles that followed. It was a rough time for me.

"On the Monday following your grandfather's burial, shortly after breakfast, I dressed and with William at my side, I guided the buggy along the road to Charles Town and my first day at the helm of, what was now Anne Cormac's businesses.

"William and I opened the door to my father's office. We began to sort through the papers on the large desk that dominated the small office. My father had often told me that his tiny office represented his beginning in Charles Town, but the large desk was to say to anyone that entered the office that he was, without question, the man in charge.

"I sat behind the desk and smiled. I was now the *woman* in charge. That smile didn't last very long. The first piece of disturbing news was that my father had borrowed a large sum of money using Goose Creek Plantation as collateral. The place I loved more than anything in the world was in jeopardy. I told William that I needed to visit the banker who held the note. I knew I would have to talk to him about the loan and some other items.

"Two blocks away on Meeting Street at the corner of Broad was the Bank of Carolina and the office of the bank's President, Richard E. Rutledge, one of my father's oldest friends. I was immediately ushered into Mr. Rutledge's office.

"He started by saying how sorry he was about my father's death. 'William Cormac was my closest friend,' he confessed.

"'That is why I am here,' I told him. 'I found this in his office this morning.' I handed the paper to Mr. Rutledge.

"He opened a desk draw and removed a folder. Over the next few minutes, Mr. Rutledge discussed what he knew about William Cormac's financial situation. 'In the last few years, your father had made a number of bad investments and the factoring business. Well, when the slave ships were bringing hundreds of slaves each month, William was very successful. He even paid for three of the ships. That was against my advice.

"One of those ships sank in bad weather. Another was stolen by the captain, a man William trusted. And the demand for slaves had diminished. William was a good man but he was far too trusting with people he did not know well enough. When the problems first started, William's savings and the profits from Goose Creek Plantation covered his losses. But losing two ships and last year's very dry season, well, let's just say I couldn't continue to provide money without collateral. That's when William pledged Goose Creek Plantation as security against the loans. I tried to convince him to cut his losses, but he was an honorable man and declared he would honor all of his commitments—even the ones to unscrupulous people who had lied to him. So you see, Miss Anne, there are money problems.'

"I started crying. William Cormac had been my strength,

my bulwark, my example. I didn't know what to do. Some moments passed. I dried my tears and asked Mr. Rutledge if he would be my financial advisor, to which he agreed.

"Back in what is now my office, William and I started going through my father's papers. Loans made by William Cormac to many of the respected citizens in Charles Town filled a drawer in the old file. Most were still unpaid. I started a list of people I needed to see for repayment.

"As the sun was dropping toward the horizon I decided it was time to return to Goose Creek Plantation. I was quiet on the trip home. I had a lot on my mind. The ability to think clearly even in desperate situations had kept me alive as a pirate on more than one occasion. I knew that quality was essential if I was going to get through this new situation.

"The evening meal was ready when I arrived home. I excused William, then ate slowly by myself. When I finished I asked for tea on the veranda. I sat in this rocking chair until well after dark. The oil lamps cast strange, frightening shadows that were a reflection of my thoughts and fears.

"I didn't sleep well that night, I remember. But the sun was shining brightly when I opened my eyes the next morning. I needed to know just how bad my financial condition was. I knew I needed a plan and I knew I would need help—help from people I could trust.

"I called for a carriage and for William. Together we headed for Charles Town and my office. We stopped at the bank on the way. I needed to talk to Mr. Rutledge. I knew he could—and probably should—demand immediate payment of my fathers debts. But I needed time. I asked him for a few weeks to get organized, so I could see exactly what my financial situation was. And I asked for his absolute silence about the matter. I knew that was the only way I could clear the mess. Thankfully, he agreed.

"William and I spent the rest of the day sorting papers and reconstructing the records of my fathers business dealings. It took two more days for me to get a handle on my needs, but at last I was able to devise a plan. The bank was my biggest creditor, since my father paid his individual creditors with money he had borrowed from the bank. William was a great help but, he while he was a man of great intelligence and unquestioned loyalty, he had few personal resources. I needed a big gun. I booked passage to Nassau.

"It was smooth sailing, and the sloop sailed into the Nassau harbor five days later. The trip gave me some extra time to consider my best path.

"When I walked into Pierre's coffee shop, he dropped a pot of coffee in surprise. The sound of that metal pot hitting the floor was deafening.

"He ran over to where I was standing. 'How have you been girl? And more important, what brings you back down here? I didn't think I'd ever see you again.'

"We embraced as only old friends do for a long moment, then I answered. 'Problems, my friend, Pierre. Problems. I needed to talk to my closest girl friend and I suppose that is you.'

"Pierre giggled. He paused long enough to slip the CLOSED sign in the window and lock the door, then he poured two cups of coffee and beckoned me to sit with him at his best table.

"For the next two hours I told Pierre my story, beginning with the last time we saw each other. I told him about my child, about my father's death, about the financial problems

I had inherited, and my immediate needs. I must tell you that the story was punctuated with bouts of tears and the caring hugs from Pierre, the Pansy Pirate.

"When I finished, a coy grin crossed Pierre's face. He had only one request. 'Tell me about the Governor's sister. I know what they said happened, but I want the real story from you.'

"I told Pierre that I would get to that, but I wanted to handle my problems. For the next hour we discussed possible alternatives, everything from Pierre fronting the money to returning to piracy and other, even more bizarre ideas, none of which were particularly practical. I didn't want to take money from Pierre. If there was one thing I learned from my father's business dealings it is that you can't borrow your way out of debt. And piracy was not an option. I'd cheated the hangman once. That was enough for me.

"At last I declared the only practical way I saw out of my current dilemma was to return to Hog Island and collect some of the treasure buried there. If it was still there.

"Pierre agreed, and together we boarded a small sloop and made the two-hour voyage to Hog Island. Truth be told, I wasn't even sure I remembered where we hid the gold. I directed the captain to a deep harbor on the on the western side of the island. I remembered there was a large sandbar that prevented ships from entering from the south, and a projection of land that provided protection from the west.

"The sandbar was in the same place as I remembered. The captain maneuvered the sloop through the small opening. We eased into the harbor area and I requested the landing boat. Pierre and I rowed the boat ashore. If the treasure was still there, I didn't want to risk having anyone see where it was hidden. The beach looked the same as I remembered it, though the trees were larger and the undergrowth more dense. I did find the location that we had chosen and was pleasantly surprised to find the treasure still intact.

"It didn't take long for us to compile a small fortune in gold. It was heavy, but Pierre and I managed to get the canvas bags back to the landing boat and get the boat back to the sloop. When the last canvas bag was safe on board the sloop, I breathed a sigh of relief.

"Pierre and I stood in the bow of the sloop letting the early evening wind to blow through our hair, though Pierre had considerably less hair to catch the wind than the last time I had seen him, and I teased him mercilessly about it. Ah, the sea air stirs the blood, I can tell you that. Once back in Nassau we transferred the gold to a sloop that Pierre had retained to take me back to Charles Town.

"We said our fare-thee-wells and the captain of my sloop made his way out of the Nassau Harbor heading back to Charles Town. I had at least three or four days with nothing to do. The sloop was well stocked by my friend Pierre, and I wanted for nothing.

"When we arrived in Charles Town around midday I sent one of the dock workers to Mr. Rutledge to request a carriage be sent to the dock. Mr. Rutledge himself, along with one of his assistants arrived with the carriage. They helped me take the gold from the sloop to my office. It was then that I realized why my father kept that large safe in his office. I transferred the gold and secured the lock and combination.

"Mr. Rutledge instructed the assistant to take him to his office and to take me to Goose Creek Plantation. I thanked the banker and told him that we would clear accounts of the next day. It seemed like a long carriage ride to Goose Creek that day."

With the skill of a master storyteller, Anne knew instinctively how to leave her audience wanting more. With a sly wink she said, "Tomorrow, Sweet Annie, I will pick up the story of solving my financial problems, and the story about your mother and the brightest day of my life—the day your mother left you here with me."

Anne doused the lanterns and the pair left their spots on the veranda. Back in her bedroom, Anne moved a chair near the window. It was a clear night and the stars were out, watching over Goose Creek Plantation. Anne's thoughts drifted back over her life. Yes, there had been dark days and weary nights, but she had been blessed with the luck of the Irish—that's how she put it.

At each low point something happened to change her life for the better. When John Bonny lied to her and took her to Nassau, Calico Jack Rackham helped her become a success in piracy. When she was convicted of piracy and sentenced to hang, her father bought her freedom. When her father died leaving her an estate in near bankruptcy, her friend Pierre and hidden gold from pirating days saved this beautiful plantation and her position. Even her daughter's stubbornness provided her with the apple of her eye, Sweet Annie.

The luck of the Irish.

It was then that she remembered something the preacher said at her father's funeral—"We are here through Divine Providence. When a door is closed, another door will open."

Perhaps it was Divine Providence that had directed her life after all, that brought her to Charles Town, gave her Goose Creek Plantation, provided her friendship with

Pierre, Calico Jack, and Mary, and placed Sweet Annie in her life.

The smile that took control of her face telegraphed her thoughts. Divine Providence or the luck of the Irish—which ever it was had made her life at this moment... perfect.

With that thought firmly pinned in her mind and the smile still on her face, she moved to her bed. The sheets made her feel the way her face looked. She took one more reassuring look at the stars, closed her eyes and slipped quickly into a dreamless sleep.

Chapter 19

The sun rose over Goose Creek Plantation, just as it had since before the area had a name. Work on the plantation started as it had for many years. The aroma of fresh coffee waggled it's index finger under the nose of the grand lady of Goose Creek. Anne Cormac rose to meet the day, just as she had for years. The remnants of the smile still lingered on her face.

Anne used the chamber pot, poured some water in the china bowl that was her sink and sponged the night sweat from her body. Ready to start her day, Anne selected comfortable clothes. She had already decided to spend at least the morning in the barn. She loved being with the animals, and she knew there was always something she could do.

Annie was already at the breakfast table when Anne arrived. She, too, was dressed in her comfortable work clothes, almost as if the two like-minded women had discussed their wardrobe the night before.

First, coffee, fried eggs, and toast, then together they headed to the barn.

They stopped by the colt's stall. He wasn't little any more, but still frisky. They stood watching the colt for several long moments before Sweet Annie broke the silence..

"I can't wait to ride him."

"I predict he will bring you years of happiness," her grandmother responded. "I have always treasured the time I have spent on horseback here at Goose Creek. I know it was the same every time I rode, but each time it seemed different, fresh and new. New sounds, new colors, new growth. Different—every time."

The rest of the morning was spent feeding animals, moving hay, cleaning out stalls. There were slaves who carried out these menial tasks each day, but they knew that *Missy Anne* liked to work with her hands, so they kept a respectful distance.

The Goose Creek ladies were called for the noon meal. Following lunch William brought the books for Anne to review. Annie remained at the big table as the numbers were reviewed. Once the figures were tallied and balanced, Anne asked William to have the horses readied. She and Annie were going to ride the fields.

It was a practice Anne had learned from her father. He had told her that riding the fields was good for the bottom line. She remembered what he said, like it was yesterday.

"You ride the fields with no schedule and no specific purpose. It is good for your laborers to see you taking interest in what they are doing. Be sure to stop and ask questions. Even if you know the answer, it is good to show you are interested and checking."

Anne continued that practice after his death, and passed the wisdom on to her granddaughter.

The evening meal was ready by the time they returned. The pair quickly changed into their evening clothes for the meal, and once satisfied, settled into their accustomed places on the veranda.

"As I recall," Anne began, "I left the story after we had put the gold in the safe."

Annie nodded, bright-eyed and eager to hear more.

"Well, the next morning William and I returned to the office to take inventory of what I had brought from Hog Island. Based on our calculations, I would be able to pay the bank loan with a sizable amount left over. I can tell you that made me feel much better. We took the gold to the bank. I told Mr. Rutledge that I had borrowed it from a wealthy friend in Nassau.

"I'm sure Mr. Rutledge knew of my adventures, but to his credit, he never expressed any doubt about where the money came from.

"My debt to the bank settled, and Goose Creek Plantation once again secure, I returned to my office and began writing letters to my father's debtors—who were now in debt to me—requesting repayment of the money my father had loaned. Fifteen letters were written, and William hand-delivered each one so there would be no doubt of them being received. The money wasn't necessary now, but clearing the ledger was. I intended to be on equal footing with the businessmen I would be dealing with.

"Mr. Rutledge made some sound suggestions, which I implemented. On his advice I decided to open my office only three hours a day, in the afternoon, and only during week days. Morning hours would then be free to concentrate on the operation of the plantation. Mr. Rutledge also suggested that I analyze the disparate businesses my father had established and discontinue any that weren't profitable. He specifically recommended closing the largely unprofitable factoring business, which I had already decided to do, but it was reassuring to hear his confirmation of my decision. It was all good advice.

"Now, back to the letters. The largest sum of money, recorded as 4,000 English pounds, was owed by one of my father's best friends, former Governor, James Moore, and he was the first to come to my office after he received my letter. I hadn't seen him since the funeral. Meeting with him was an important part of assuming control of my father's businesses. He agreed with the number and suggested he pay the debt with some land and a few slaves, and pay the remainder in cash spread out over a few months. We came to an agreement. He departed as a friend and remains a confident.

"About half of the letters resulted in visits from indignants—men who tried to say they didn't owe the money, or that they had already repaid the debts, or who were insulted that a *girl* would make demands of them. I had little patience with these men. They all got the same answer—pay up or expect an invitation to visit the Royal Court.

"All paid but one—an arrogant farmer named Tradd. He stormed into my office and declared he had never worked with a young girl and he never would. He insisted since my father was dead, his debt was negated.

"I told him otherwise and demanded payment.

"He stormed out the same way as he entered. The upshot of it all is, we went to court and he was required to pay the debt.

"I learned that there were many businessmen, like many pirates, who refused to deal with women. But the strategies that worked as a pirate, also worked with a businessmen—not the kneeing them in the nutmegs part, but by being fair and hard. Soon my reputation as a hard but fair businesswoman became widely known and respected. With all of the money repaid and the treasure brought from Nassau, Goose Creek

Plantation was now secure and there was capital available to operate it successfully.

"But now, the story returns to your mother. She was 15 years old when we sent her to the Old Country to complete her education. She was 17 when she returned—still impertinent, disrespectful, and impossible to live with. She refused to take directions from anyone, especially now that her grandfather was dead.

"And she was pregnant. She claimed to have no idea who the father was. The servants we had sent to accompany her and to keep her out of that kind of trouble begged for my forgiveness and even asked to be punished for their lack of vigilance. I knew my daughter well enough to know a battalion of servants would not have been able to control her. She was too much like me at that age. I forgave the servants, but dismissed them from my service.

"I had a meeting with your mother. We reached an accord. She would remain at Goose Creek Plantation until you were born. She agreed to not create any problems, and in return for her cooperation I would provide her with a sizable bank account. She could leave Goose Creek after the birth as soon as she could travel, but with the caveat that if she left, she would leave without you and she would be on her own and could expect no more help from me. I would raise the child as my own.

"One month and two weeks later, a horse left Goose Creek Plantation carrying Mary Cormac and all of her worldly goods. That was 18 years ago. She never returned."

The older woman pursed her lips, and stared into the distance. The silence that followed was complete, save for the sounds of spirituals being sung from the slave quarters, and the natural sounds of crickets and bullfrogs. Neither woman spoke for a long moment.

At last Anne breathed softly, "This has been a strange day. I was reliving the—" She paused then let out a deep sigh. "I was reliving the years I spent here with your mother. I've come to believe that everything she did was to make me pay for what I had done to my father. I named her Mary after the two most important women in my life—Mary Brennan, my mother and your great grandmother, and Mary Reid, my friend, my shipmate, and my cellmate.

"I remember the evening before your mother left. She called me everything but white, and blamed me for all of the things that had gone wrong in her life. She left the next morning. I was like a ship on a stormy sea—up and down, up and down; happy she was leaving, sad she was leaving.

"Finally, William—now remember, he was still a slave—said 'Let's go to the veranda and talk.' I respected his request. I sat right where you are sitting and William sat where I am sitting. I didn't know what to say. The silence was a pall that hung over both of us. He started the conversation by saying, 'Everything has happened for the best. Mary now has the opportunity to make the most of her life. She has an education and a substantial bank account. Whatever the outcome, it is now her choice.'

"I said I felt like it was my fault that she turned out as she did. He said it wasn't my fault, but even if I were responsible, there was nothing more I could do except allow her to make her own decisions.

"He stood and looked at me. 'Pardon me Missy Anne, but your father is gone. He educated you to run a successful plantation. He put all of his knowledge into your head. But he's gone now, and this place is your'n. You need to run it for yourself and for that beautiful little girl in your arms. You're prepared and you can do it.'

"It was unheard of for a slave to speak so directly to his owner, but it was William's frank advice that put things in perspective. He knew I needed a—as he called it—'a good talking to.'

"The next day I called all of the servants, slaves, and hired hands together for a meeting at noon meal. I wanted everyone to hear what I had to say, and I didn't want anyone to rely on what someone else said I said.

"I started my conversation with my heartfelt feelings. 'First of all, I want you to know that you are the heart and soul of Goose Creek Plantation. My father built this farm into the successful business it is today with the active involvement of each of you. I plan to continue his work. I learned the business of running this plantation at his elbow, and I know that you loved him, almost as much as I did. Today is no different than yesterday, a year ago, or a year in the future. We all have work to do, and we will stay one big happy family as long as everyone does his or her work. That is my plan.'

"And that is what we did."

There was a lull in the story, and Annie took advantage to interject. "Granny Anne, you said you would tell me about your conversation with your father about your release from prison."

Anne leaned way back in the rocking chair. She gazed at the stars for some time as if she were deciding what she would say or how she would say it.

"Your great grandfather was a man of few words. When I arrived back in Charles Town, it was a short carriage ride from the dock to the house. I didn't know what to say or how to start. My father stopped the carriage. He leaned close to me, put his arms around me, and started crying. It was the first time I had ever seen him cry. I never saw him shed a tear, not even when my mother died. I was crying too. It took us a few minutes to gather our emotions. He held my shoulders at arm's length, looked me in the eye, and said, 'Daughter, I love you with all my heart.' That was another first. I don't recall him ever before telling me he loved me. You look so much like your mother. When she died you were my life. 'I had planned so much for her and for you. I loved you even through those trying years when you were growing up. I knew you were hurting but I didn't know what to do because I was hurting, too. When you left, I thought you would come to your senses, come back home with me. When you didn't my life became this plantation and my businesses. I was as successful in business as I was a failure with my family.'

"He started crying again. The hug that followed was a catharsis for both of us. The hug was so tight it was painful, releasing the pain we had caused each other. He whispered in my ear, 'I love you, daughter. I love you, Anne. I love you.'

"I told him that I loved him too. I suppose that was the first time I ever told him that I loved him. 'I love you, too.' That's what I whispered to him. Such simple words, so long overdue.

"At some point he was able to regain control of his emotions. He straightened up, wiped my tears with the handkerchief he always carried, then wiped his own. 'What's past is past,' he pronounced. 'There is a lot more to say, daughter, but enough for now. We need to get you home. We can decide what to do for you and for your baby tomorrow.' With that we continued the ride to this house.

"I saw him cry only one more time. That was the day when your mother left for England.

"There's a lot more to say, but this is enough for now. I'm weary. I must go to bed."

The mistress and the heiress of Goose Creek Plantation climbed the stairs, each heading for their respective bedrooms. Anne was lost in thoughts. She hugged her granddaughter goodnight, perhaps a bit longer than usual.

"I love you, Sweet Annie. I love you. Sleep well."

Anne stripped off the residue of the emotions she had re-experienced as she stripped off her clothes. The chair was still by the window where she had left it the night before. It was another clear night and her faithful stars were right where she had left them.

She eased into her comfortable chair and started a mental conversation with her stars. She told them about her day, about reliving the day her father said he loved her, about the many times she had hurt her father and how much she missed the Marys in her life—mother, daughter, and friend.

She was busy telling them of her regrets for all of the failures of being Mary's mother when they decided they had heard enough. They directed the sleep fairy to end the conversation, for in their starry wisdom they knew that sleep was the answer to all of those problems. What was done was done and couldn't be undone. Anne had a second chance—Annie.

Hours later Anne managed to rouse herself enough to trade the comfortable chair for a comfortable bed.

Chapter 20

It was Sunday morning, and the Goose Creek Plantation ladies did as they did on most Sundays. Anne went to Annie's bedroom to awaken her, but she found the young girl already getting ready for church. The pair met at the carriage for the ride to St. Phillips Episcopal Church. It was a new building in the center of Charles Town. The building was constructed with a sizable donation form Anne Cormac.

The trip to the town was uneventful. Anne received numerous invitations to join families for Sunday dinner. She thanked each one graciously, but declined. She retrieved their buggy and directed the horse toward White Point Gardens. From where she stopped the buggy, she and Annie could see the beginning of the ocean that separated America from England. Not too far to the south was the Straits of Florida, Nassau, Jamaica, Cuba, and the waters around other islands where Anne made her reputation. Not more than a hundred feet was the place where her friend, Stede Bonnet, the Gentleman Pirate, was hanged. This wasn't the first time she had visited this spot, but it was the first time with Annie.

"That tree was where Stede was hanged." She pointed so Annie would know what she was saying. "That tree. He was a good man and a good pirate. But, like Jack, he let his guard down and he was captured."

With that, she snapped the reigns and brought the horse to life. They rode down the street by the water, by the docks, by the slave market, by the office that now served as Anne's business home, and onto the road that led to Goose Creek Plantation. Anne didn't say anything until she turned the horse onto the tree-lined avenue that led to the plantation house. Once she could see the house she said to Annie, "I have always loved this view of the plantation house. I think it looks like me. Steady, strong, but not pretentious."

Noon meal had been prepared and awaited their arrival. They removed their hats before they moved to the table, but remained dressed in their church clothes. As they ate, Anne kept the conversation light. They discussed the clothing the other ladies were wearing. They discussed the minister's sermon, the beauty of White Point, and the ocean. They finished the meal in silence. It was as if Anne were deciding what they should do next.

"Let's go to the veranda," Anne said. She asked for tea to be served there, and she led Annie to their recognized conversation place.

"And so, Sweet Annie, you now know most of my story. For the last 17 years you have been a part of that story. You were everything I had wanted Mary to be. You are as capable of running this plantation as I am—or was. You have become a genteel lady at the times you need to be a lady, and strong, powerful woman when that was needed. I am so proud of you, and I am confident that you will run the empire that your great grandfather started and built, and which I have grown.

"The Cormac name is on only one building in Charles Town—Cormac Theater. But Cormac money is silently behind much of the culture of Charles Town. The Charles Town Library Society, the third oldest in the country, was started by a few friends when I said I would back it. Charles

Town's fire insurance company was started shortly after my office was damaged in 1740. And St. Michael Church couldn't have been built without Cormac money.

"But that is how I wanted it. I wanted to be in the background. That is the Cormac way. I hope it is the way you will be when you are in control.

"There you have it, child, the story you asked for—The absolutely true story of Anne Bonny, the world's first female pirate."

"What happened to James, Granny Anne?"

"I don't know, Sweet Annie." Anne paused for a long moment. "I don't know, but he changed his loyalty with the whims of the wind. I expect he was killed by someone he crossed. I once thought I loved him, but he turned out to be a spineless bastard. From the time I met Calico Jack Rackham, he became the only man I truly loved. But when he lost his backbone I realized the only person I could trust was me. Until I came back home, and realized the one man who truly loved me for myself, was the one man I had fought so hard to get away from—my father."

Mist clouded the older woman's eyes, and Annie turned to stare into the distance, giving her grandmother time to recover her emotions.

"Now," Anne said at last. "It's time for you to tell me what you want for your birthday."

Chapter 21

As the sloop sails silently away from the dock at Goose Creek Plantation, two figures were silhouetted against the blue, violet, red, orange, and yellow that blended to create the sunrise sky.

"Are you sure this is the only thing you want for your birthday?"

"I'm sure," Annie replied. "But, are you ready for this, Granny Anne?" With those words Sweet Annie stripped off her waistcoat and stood, proudly next to her Grandmother with the morning breeze blowing softly across her bare breasts.

Anne smiled broadly as she stood next to her granddaughter. She grabbed her waistcoat and ripped it open.

"I suppose I am," she laughed.

"Granny Anne. I do have one other small birthday wish. Would you please just call me Annie?"

The older woman nodded and gazed into the rising sun. "Alright. Annie it is."

A moment of silence followed.

"And, you can call me Anne."

Timeline

1698–Anne is born in Kensale, County Cork, Ireland
1699–Cormac family moves from Kensale to Charles Town
1703–William Cormac hired by Col. Rhett
1706–Cormac buys Goose Creek Plantation
1707–Anne beats up boy at school
1708–Mary Brennan (Anne's mother) dies
1709–Anne stabs servant girl
1713–Hurricane causes heavy flooding 70 people killed
1714–Anne marries James Bonny
1714–The Bonny's move to New Providence (Nassau)
1718–November 22 Pirate Edward Teach (Blackbeard) dies from syphilis most likely
1718–November 24 Pirate Calico Jack Rackham voted in as captain
1718–November 26 Pirate Stede Bonnet hanged at low water mark White Point in Charles Town
1719–August Anne Bonny's first pirate adventure with Jack Rackham
1720–November 15 Anne, Mary Reid and Jack Rackham were captured
1720–November 18 Calico Jack Rackham hanged
1720–November 28 Anne and Mary were sentenced to hang

1721–Anne returns to Charles Town and Goose Creek Plantation

1721–Mary Bonny was born

1735–Mary sent to England

1736–Cormac Theater Built

1737–William Cormac dies

1738–Mary returns to Charleston and Goose Creek Plantation

1738–Annie Cormac is born

1738–Mary leaves Goose Creek Plantation.

1740–Fire destroys water front district and damages Ann's office

1748–Charleston Library Society organized with Anne Cormac

1750–Charles Town, now Charleston, wealthiest and largest city south of Philadelphia

PIRATE LEXICON

Abbess–the mistress of a brothel

Batchelor's son–a bastard

Careen–clean seaweed and barnacles from the bottom of a ship

Dirk–a long, thin knife used for fighting in close quarters

Dirty Puzzle–a nasty slut

Gomorrhean–male homosexual

Hanging Cabin–a hammock usually for common sailors

Inch of Candle–A time limit. Usually used in auctions high bid plus a Inch of Candle would seal the bid.

Jack Kecth–the hangman as in "dance with Jack Kecth" or "cheat Jack Kecth"

King Turniphead–King George II
Kilkenny Cat–
Kill Devil–
miculo–Spanish for "my ass"
Molly House–meeting place for homosexual men
Monkey–small cannon
Mum–ale made from wheat and oats flavored with herbs.
No Prey No Pay–crew received no wages only a percentage of the loot
Nutmegs–testicles, balls
On The Account–a pirate who had signed the Articles of Agreement
Punch House–English term for brothel or low-class drinking pub
Salmagundi–also called Solomon Grundy resembled a chefs salad—bits of marinated fish, turtle and other meats combined with herbs, palm hearts, spiced wine and oil, boiled eggs, pickled onions, cabbage, grapes, and olives, or any combination that was available.
Scurvy–a disease caused by lack of vitamin C or a term that meant vile, mean, contemptible.
Trot–decrepit old woman
Widdles–food

PIRATE WEIGHTS AND MEASURES

Money–The "coin of the realm" in Carolina in pirate days was the English Pound. 1 pound was worth about $80 in today's money.
Measurements–Pirates did not have rulers of measuring tape so, for a pirate, measurements had to be made with what was available, their bodies.

a fathom–roughly the height of a pirate so, approximately 6 feet

one yard–the distance between the tip of your nose and the end of your fingers with an arm outstretched

one cubit–the distance between your elbow and the tip of your finger (approximately 18 inches)

one foot–the length of a human foot (approximately 12 inches)

one hand–the distance between the tip of the thumb and the tip of the little finger of a hand with the fingers spread (approximately 4 inches)

one inch–the distance of the middle bone of the index finger (approximately 1 inch)

Storage Containers–Barrels were the common storage containers and they were made by "coopers". A cooper had standards for the barrels they made based on the volume they carried. Larger ships often included a cooper among their crew more as a necessity that a luxury.

a puncheon–either 84 or 120 gallons depending on contents being shipped

a butt–108 gallon cask

a hogshead–63 gallon cask

a barrel–between 31 and 42 gallons

a tierce–42 gallons

a kilderkin–18 gallons

a firkin–9 gallons

a rundlet–between 3 and 20 gallons but usually 14.5 gallons

PIRATE RECIPES

Grog–the most simple mixture called grog was rum mixed with water and some lemon or lime juice. A proper grog, however, was rum and water that contained a generous portion of lime juice to stave off scurvy and a measure of cane sugar to kill the bitterness of the water.

1 oz of rum

the juice of half a lime

one to two teaspoons cane sugar

water to fill your tin (cup) or mug.

Hardtack–the equivalent of bread on pirate ships because it could be stocked without spoiling.

2 cups flour

1/2 teaspoon salt

1/2 to 3/4 cup water

Preheat oven to around 250 degrees F. Combine flour and salt in a bowl. Add water and mix with hands until the dough comes together. Roll out on a table to about 1/3 inch thickness. Use a knife to cut the dough into 3" by 3" squares. Place on a baking sheet and with a sharpened dowel make 16 evenly-spaced holes in each square of dough. Bake at least 4 hours turning half through the baking. Cool in a dry room and store in a dry place.

Salmagundi–the 1700s equivalent of a chefs salad, salmagundi was any combination of roasted meat and vegetables, salad greens and cheese with lemons or limes. Fruits, such as oranges and pineapples, were a common addition. Recipes for preparing salmagundi are varied as the lists of contents. Included here are two recipes which will illustrate the point.

8–10 shrimp (shell on)

2 cloves of garlic

1/2 lemon

olive oil

salt and pepper

Toss the shrimp, garlic, olive oil, lemon juice and salt and pepper in an iron pot. Heat until shrimp are cooked through.

poached chicken breast

1 chicken breast

1 carrot (medium, diced)

1 celery (medium, diced)

2 sprigs of thyme

2 cloves garlic

1 teaspoon sea salt

Put the chicken, carrots, celery, thyme, garlic and salt in a medium saucepan. Cover with 1 inch of water. Cook over medium heat for 15 minutes until cooked through. Let cool before slicing.

heirloom tomatoes

2 large eggs boiled

olives

grapes

Serve the shrimp, slices of poached chicken, eggs, tomatoes, olives, and grapes on a large platter.

Salmagundi (from "The Good Huswives Treasure" 1588-1660)

Cut cold roast chicken and other meats into slices. Mix minced tarragon with slices of onions. Mix capers, olives, samphire, broombuds, mushrooms, oysters, lemon juice, orange juice, raisins, almonds, blue figs, Virginia potatoes, peas and red and white currents. Arrange on a plate. Garnish with slices of orange and lemon. Cover with oil and vinegar beaten together.

About the Author

Ralph E. Jarrells entered the field of writing novels late in his life. He retired from corporate America eight years ago and began an award winning video production company that specialized in creating video programs for ministry and mission organizations. So far, his work has received 18 international creative awards.

He retired from a successful career in marketing, advertising and publishing that included senior executive positions with major corporations—Sr. VP Marketing with an international franchise company, VP Marketing with a NYSE company, VP Account Supervisor for the world's largest advertising company and Editorial director for a major trade magazine publishing company.

Connect with Ralph online at:

www.illgottengain.net

Also Available From

WordCrafts Press

The Pruning
    by Jan Cline

Until Then
    by Gail Kittleson

The Sisters of Lazarus Trilogy
    by Paula K. Parker

Angela's Treasures
    by Marian Rizzo

Saturday & the Witch Woman
    by Thomas O. Ott

www.WordCrafts.net

Printed in Great Britain
by Amazon